Lake Rules

Maureen Garvie

KEY PORTER BOOKS

Library and Archives Canada Cataloguing in Publication

Garvie, Maureen
    Lake rules / Maureen Garvie.

ISBN 1-55263-672-0

I. Title.

PS8563.A6749L33 2005   jC813'.6   C2005-901211-0

The publisher gratefully acknowledges the support of the Canada Council for the Arts and the Ontario Arts Council for its publishing program. We acknowledge the support of the Government of Ontario through the Ontario Media Development Corporation's Ontario Book Initiative.

We acknowledge the financial support of the Government of Canada through the Book Publishing Industry Development Program (BPIDP) for our publishing activities.

Key Porter Books Limited
Six Adelaide Street East
Tenth Floor
Toronto, Ontario
Canada M5C 1H6

www.keyporter.com

Text design: Peter Maher
Electronic formatting: Jean Lightfoot Peters

Printed and bound in Canada

05 06 07 08 09 10 6 5 4 3 2 1

For Edna, May, Faye, Ruby and Jean Heath,
source of all the best lake rules

Acknowledgments

This book has been around in various forms for so long that my debts are many. Johanne Greenhow and I began it in Miss Muirhead's French class, continuing it in Miss Gosling's Latin class, passing it back and forth through the school day like a long note. So thanks, Johanne, for the spark, and the tolerance.

Leila Garvie typed in the yellowed pages when they came to light, dropped the hopeless bits and read successive versions without complaint. Shelley Tanaka told me the truth. George Lovell listened to it not once but twice with unfailing graciousness and solicitous concern for Hugo's rabbit. My brother Rob went so far as to say he liked it.

My Tuesday night Ban Righ writing group—Bill Hutchinson, Kris Andrychuk, Christina Decarie, Denise Kenny and Nancy Brown—gave encouragement and insights; David Pratt and John Donaldson offered sound advice on what you can and cannot do in a canoe. Thanks also to Nina Lewis, Jessie MacDonald, and Bonnie Thompson.

To Fred Brown I owe the original of Marcel's totem, to David and Rob McCallum the originals of Tim and Hugo, to Jay and Joe Yule, the original boat on the horizon. Thanks to Nicola Matthews for the "ageing nymphomaniac" expletive and the Kingston Yacht Club for the Nutshells.

The excerpts from "At Gull Lake: August, 1810" and "Powassan's Drum" are by Duncan Campbell Scott

(1862–1947), poet and deputy superintendent of Indian Affairs.

Marijka Huitema's master's thesis for the geography department of Queen's University, "Land of Which the Savages Stood in No Particular Need," provided a clear-eyed picture of the Algonkins living in the area of my fictional Lake Wasamak.

And thanks especially to Linda Pruessen for guiding the book smoothly and expertly to publication.

Lake Rules

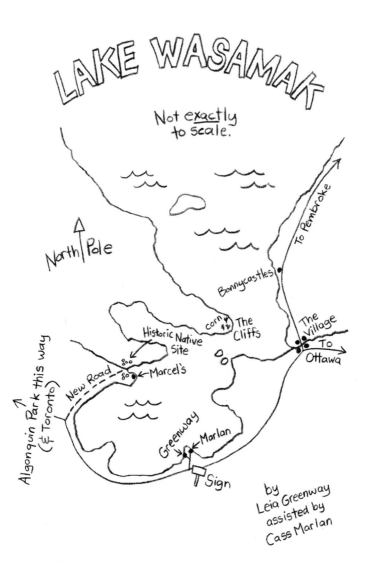

Prologue

————— ➷ —————

THE COTTAGE WAS EXACTLY how I'd pictured it, half hidden in the pines, dark green with a big stone chimney. It looked a little neglected and forlorn.

We trudged up the hill from the car, weighed down with groceries, and Mom stuck out her hand with the keys. "Who's going to open the door?"

I grabbed them before either of my brothers could. "I will!" I'd been waiting for this moment forever. I was so excited I dropped all my bags.

Fumbling with the lock, I peered through the front door window. Inside, the cottage was dim and shadowy, with humps of furniture and dark pictures on the walls. But out through the big window at the back I could see Lake Wasamak, all bright and glittering blue.

And right then I had a very weird experience. Maybe it was a hallucination—after all, I'd been imagining this day for a whole school year. Or maybe it was from being in the car so long, like when you stand up too fast and everything goes black and starry. But for an instant, when those two windows lined up, I saw things—like pictures on a screen, like a dream in fast-forward. I saw sun glinting off water, paddles dipping, people laughing and eating, campfires burning. It all happened so fast, like my life flashing in front of my eyes—except it wasn't my life but other lives, lots of lives. I felt a rush of joy and wild exhilaration, feelings so wonderful they took my breath away. And then darkness closed in around the edges, and a terrible sadness.

And then I was just standing in front of the cottage door with my brothers and mother behind me: Leia, an ordinary thirteen-year-old girl on a warm, sunny day in May.

I guess there could be a scientific explanation—the way those windows lined up, maybe, like the lenses in a camera, catching particles of memory between them. Anyway, I've looked through those very same windows plenty of times since, and it's never happened again.

Lots of other incredible things happened, though.

One

———————➤———————

"LEIA! WAKE UP AND OPEN THE DOOR!" Tim snapped. "My arms are dropping off."

"And a million bugs are biting me," whined Hugo.

But the key wouldn't work. I tried it again. Maybe it was the wrong key. Maybe we wouldn't be able to get in and we'd have to drive all the way back to Toronto.

"Let me try, Leia," Mom said. Just then the key turned, and the door opened with a groan. A breath of musty-smelling air rolled past us.

My mind and body were numb from six hours in the car. All I'd had to eat were three chocolate doughnuts and a disgusting blend of Orange Crush, Diet Coke and Dr Pepper. What can I say? It seemed like a good idea at the time. The car's air-conditioning had stopped working around Oshawa. For the first little while, the fresh air was nice, but the last part of the drive was on winding gravel roads. Pretty soon we were all coughing from the dust streaming in through the windows. Hugo threw up twice. Now he was peering into the cottage, clutching his rabbit in her cage. "I'm not taking Rover in there. There might be weasels."

"Out of my way, then." Mom moved us aside and strode in fearlessly. A minute later the overhead light went on. "No weasels. Rover's quite safe."

Hugo and Tim pushed past me over the doorstep. I took a deep breath and followed. A deer with spreading antlers stared down at us from over the fireplace.

"Hey, it's Bambi's father," said Tim.

Hugo blinked. "Where's the rest of him?" I could see the wheels turning in his eight-year-old brain. He probably thought the deer's back end was on the other side of the wall.

"That's all there is. They cut his head off and stuffed it," Tim said.

A look of horror crossed Hugo's face. "That's gross!"

While we stood there contemplating Bambi's poor dad, Mom started pulling back curtains and letting in light. The place was old and cozy, like Gran's cottage used to be. The big room with the fireplace had comfortable chairs and couches, and the ceiling was wood, like the floor. There were shelves all around packed with ancient paperbacks and magazines.

Mom was good at thinking ahead. She'd arranged for somebody from the village to come and hook up the plumbing, but things in the kitchen didn't look too hopeful. "Here goes nothing," she said and turned the tap. Rusty water gargled out, but after a few coughs and spits it miraculously started running clear.

Next to the kitchen was a hallway that led to a back door and bedrooms. "Where do we sleep, Mom?" I asked her.

"Yours is the little room next to the bathroom. The one with the bunks is the boys'."

I wished my room had bunks. I always wanted to sleep in the top bunk, even when there was nobody on the bottom. But the boys had to share their room, and I got one all to myself, even if it was small. Mom's bedroom was way on the other side of the living room.

A door on the other side of the kitchen opened onto a big screened porch. It had a table and a rocking chair where you could sit and look at the water, safe from the mosquitoes. I walked outside, sat in the chair and took a deep breath of spring air. The lake was hardly ten feet away. It was so still and quiet—not a boat or cottage in sight. For a moment, it felt like we were the only people on the planet. I looked at my watch and thought about Toronto and how the rush-hour fumes from Eglinton Avenue would soon be drifting into our apartment. It was the hottest, most humid May I could remember, but then again, it was the first one I'd ever had to spend in the city. Here, though, the air was practically green with oxygen. When I listened for cars, all I heard were crows cawing.

And Hugo complaining. "Yuck! Mom, there's about a foot of mouse droppings in here. Where are some traps?"

"We'll get traps," said Mom, as I walked back into the kitchen. "And the rest of the wildlife is going, too. That deer over the mantel, and the stuffed fish." She pointed to two big pike with glassy eyes, mounted on the living-room wall. One was losing its stuffing.

"You can't throw those out," Tim protested. "They're antiques."

"That deer keeps staring at me," said Hugo.

"They're all out of here," Mom said. She started issuing orders about unloading the car.

"Why can't Leia do it?" Hugo said. "Me and Tim are invalids."

"Tim is excused on health grounds. But a little exercise won't hurt you, Hugo." Mom grabbed Hugo and started slathering him with sunblock and insect repellant while he squirmed. She passed me the bottles. "Don't either of you go wandering off. By the time anyone found you, you'd be gnawed to the bone by blackflies." She called after us through the back door, "Just stack my paints outside my studio. And see if you can find a hammer so we can put the screens on."

15

The car was parked down the hill by the boathouse. Hugo trudged ahead of me through a tunnel of pine boughs. "You'd have to drop dead to get out of being a slave around here," he grumbled. "I want to explore."

"Quit complaining. We could be in school doing math right now." I loaded him with bags of swim fins and towels from the trunk. The hammer turned up in a box with pasta and sheets.

"Yeah, Pamela Anderson fractions. Top half bigger than the bottom." Hugo snorted. A supply teacher, an old guy of at least fifty, had said that to my class once as a joke. I made the mistake of telling Hugo. Perfect eight-year-old humor.

"So quit complaining," I said again. The only thing I cared about was that we were here.

After all, it had taken some pretty heavy-duty lobbying. I'd stuck photos of the cottage all over the fridge. I'd thumbtacked a map of Ontario to the kitchen board, with a big red arrow pointing to the spot. Every night before I went to sleep, I conjured up the image of a cool lake under blue sky, clouds like fluffy dumplings reflected in the water. A breeze ruffling the surface. *Wasamak*, it whispered. *Wasamak*.

My wish had come finally true. I figured I was owed one, after a bunch of major disasters. My parents got divorced, my gran had to go into a nursing home, and Mom moved me and my brothers to the city. Anyway, we were out of there now, and it was just too bad that Tim and Hugo had to get sick for it to happen.

It had all been terrible: Mom talking on the phone every night to Dad in a voice so low I couldn't hear, and Tim in the hospital for three days. When Mom came back from taking him there, she looked totally wiped. Her hair was sticking up, and she didn't seem to know or care that she'd been walking around Toronto with a big smear of green paint on her cheek.

She sank into a chair. "Chicken pox! Oh, Leia, I feel dreadful. I thought Hugo was just making a big fuss over a rash. Even when Tim started to look so awful, I didn't think it was serious. I only called the doctor because he got it on his tongue. They told me at the hospital it could have spread to his internal organs. That would have been very serious."

I had a sudden vision of my brothers lying side by side, pale and still, arms folded on their chests. I clutched Mom's hand. "They couldn't die, could they?"

She shook her head. "No, honey, they'll be fine. Tim's on some heavy-duty medication now, and the hospital staff are keeping him under observation. He might even be able to come home tomorrow."

"Is that what they said?"

She nodded, and I let my breath out again.

"The spots will just take time to go away," she went on. "The boys will be out of school until June, which really means until the end of the term. It won't be a problem for Hugo, but I don't want Tim losing his first year of high school."

I didn't get chicken pox because I was immune. Mom said I had them when I was little. Hugo got better pretty quickly, except for being cranky and itchy. But when Tim came home from the hospital, I got a lump in my stomach every time I looked at him. Hugo's chest and stomach were spotty, but Tim looked like a cranberry muffin all over.

He knew how bad he looked, too, and he didn't want anybody to see him. He stayed in his room with his door shut, watching his old TV. The color didn't really work on it anymore, so everything was green. That's okay for nature programs, but it's not so good for hockey. It had

17

never bothered Tim, though, because before he got sick he didn't watch much TV. He was always doing stuff—taking his bike apart, going off to soccer, fooling around on the computer with his new friends. Now he just lay around looking like the Curse of the Red Death.

"The virus has put a lot of stress on his system," Mom said, when I asked if he'd ever get back to normal. "It doesn't help that he's growing so much. Poor Tim."

After a couple of days of being shut up in the apartment with the two boys, Mom wasn't nearly so sympathetic. She was trying to get some paintings ready for a one-woman show in September, and she still had tons to do. "I need to have more than five new pieces finished—it's been three years since my last solo show. But how am I supposed to work with those two in my space all the time?"

"Can't they go and stay with Dad in Port Hope?" I asked.

She reminded me that Dad was going to be in New Brunswick. He's an engineer, and he was starting a six-week contract there.

Then it hit me—my most brilliant idea ever. "We can all go to the cottage early!"

Mom shot it down without a second thought. "I don't think you should miss so much school."

"It's just a few weeks, Mom, and it's only grade seven. It's not like I'll be missing anything important. All we'll be doing is watching videos and cleaning out the art cupboards."

"You might not like this cottage when you actually get there," she warned. She was the only one who'd seen it so far, when she went up in the fall to buy it. It was way up north, almost in Quebec, on a lake that had an Indian name: Wasamak. I loved the sound of it.

"Do Indians live there?" I asked, daydreaming a little.

"Not anymore, I don't think. But it's certainly back-woods. The mosquitoes will be terrible this early in the season. And there's no satellite dish, so TV reception will be lousy. And you'll be away from all your friends."

I didn't mind. I had some sort-of friends at my new school, but not like the ones I used to have in Port Hope. Hugo and Tim couldn't see any of their friends anyway, stuck in an apartment with chicken pox. So the cottage sounded perfect to me.

After we finished unpacking the car, Mom made us a late lunch—grilled cheese sandwiches and chocolate milk. We ate out on the screened porch, with Rover grazing underfoot for crumbs. Hugo doused his sandwich with ketchup, his favorite vegetable. Tim didn't have much of an appetite. He'd lost a lot of weight, though you could hardly tell with his cap pulled down and his collar pushed up.

Mom carried her dishes to the sink and got out a broom and dustpan. "I haven't even had a chance to see how the renovations on my studio turned out. Come out when you've finished cleaning up. There should be plenty of hot water now for doing dishes."

Tim and Hugo groaned.

"Once she gets painting, she'll forget about us," I said. "Then we can do what we like."

But when we went to see the shed that was supposed to be converted into Mom's studio, we found her stand-ing ankle deep in wood shavings, looking like she wanted to cry.

"It's a disaster," she said, shoving her fingers through her hair. "The carpenters promised me it would be ready, but it's nowhere near done." She caught Hugo by his hood as he tried to push past her into the empty space. "Watch where you step. The floorboards are so thin you could fall through. And those men were smoking in here." Cigarette butts were mixed with the nails and wood and sawdust on the floor.

"Guess they're still working on it," Tim said.

She gazed around hopelessly. "I can't paint in here."

"Don't worry, Mom," Hugo said soothingly. "It's okay."

But it wasn't. She'd been planning her studio all winter: where the windows would be, how many shelves she'd need, where her workbench would go. No wonder she was upset.

"The boathouse down by the car is ours, isn't it?" Tim asked after a minute. "Why can't you use that for your studio?"

She shook her head. "There's not enough light with all those trees. Besides, it's full of junk. No, this would have been perfect, except it's ruined. This whole venture is beginning to seem like a bad idea." She squared her shoulders. "I need another cup of tea. I'm going to have to rethink things." She walked back to the cottage.

Rethink things? That sounded ominous. I looked around. "What a mess. That big window is so crooked it looks like it's going to fall on us."

Tim went outside. "They've just stuck it in temporarily." I could hear him talking as clearly as if he was in the room. "It could be straightened."

"Maybe those guys will come back and do it."

"I only need to raise the corner."

"You don't know how, Tim. Besides, you don't have any tools."

"There's a hammer. And Mom's got screwdrivers and vise grips in her framing kit."

He came back in and pawed through the garbage on

the floor, collecting scraps of wood. The methodical way he was doing it reminded me of Dad. Tim looks like Dad, too—a lot skinnier, but tall, with the same sandy hair. Me and Hugo are more like Mom, short and dark.

I stared at the back of his neck. "Your spots don't look so bad now."

"Shut up."

"No, really. They're not as purple as they were."

"I look like dried lava, and the itching is driving me nuts." He grabbed the broom, stuck the handle under one edge of the window and levered it up. Then he told me to wedge in one of the pieces of wood he'd picked up.

"How do you know how to do this?"

"Dad."

I remembered then how he used to help Dad build things all the time. "You don't think Mom's going to change her mind and make us go back home, do you?"

"She might."

"But she can't paint at home either! That's why we came."

He shrugged. "Stick in another wood shim." Every time I added one, he pulled the broom out and stood back to see if the window was straight. "We really need a level, but that looks okay to me," he said finally. "I just need to nail on some trim to hold it in place." He started picking up loose boards and leaning them against the wall, long ones at one end and short ones at the other. "Some of these might do it."

"Don't you need a saw?"

"They left us one." He kicked at something on the floor, then pulled it from the sawdust. It looked rusty.

I reached for the broom. "This place will look lots better if it's cleaned up. Hugo can pick up the nails."

Speaking of Hugo, where was he? I ran back to the

cottage to look for him, but he wasn't there—only Mom, rubbing on insect repellant to go for a walk. "Everything okay, Leia?" she asked.

"Sure, Mom, you go ahead." I watched her stroll over the hill and out of sight before I went down the path in the other direction. Hugo wasn't near the car or by the boathouse either. I called his name, but not too loud. I didn't want Mom to hear.

Then I heard something. A voice, shouting.

"Here! I'm over here!"

And out in the bay, in the middle of the clear-blue afternoon, was Hugo. In a boat.

Two

"WHERE'D HE GET THAT?" Tim was behind me, staring like he couldn't believe his eyes.

The boat was sitting weirdly low in the water and Hugo was frantically scooping handfuls over the side. When he saw us on shore, he stood up and waved.

"Help!" He sounded scared. "Hey, you guys! Help, I'm sinking!" With the boat rocking wildly now and his arms windmilling, Hugo grabbed for the side to keep from falling. The boat tipped one way. Hugo threw himself the other.

"Hugo!" I screamed. The boat was upside down, and I couldn't see Hugo at all.

If he drowned, it would be all my fault. I was the one who wanted to come here. I should have been keeping an eye on my little brother.

"Hugo!"

His head came up. It swiveled, looking around for the boat, which was wallowing a few yards away. He dog-paddled toward it, churning the surface, with his neck stretched. That water was like ice.

When he stopped, he wasn't any nearer to the boat than when he'd started. Last summer he'd had swimming lessons, but they didn't seem to be working. His head disappeared again.

Tim pulled his sweatshirt off. His chest was very skinny and covered in dark crusty spots. "Hang on, Hugo, I'm coming!"

"You're not, Tim!" I grabbed his belt. "You'll get pneumonia!"

He shook me off angrily. "Hugo's drowning!"

"He's not. Look." Hugo's head was above water again. "He's waving!"

"Can you touch bottom?" Tim yelled to him.

"Yes, but—" Hugo sank once more. He bobbed back up, sputtering. "I can't keep my head out of the water and touch bottom at the same time." Down he went again.

"Help!" he croaked on his next bob. He must have got a mouthful, because he began to cough.

Tim waded in. I tried to pull my shoes off and grab him at the same time. As we struggled on the shore, a red canoe appeared around the point.

Hugo saw it, too. "Help!" he shrieked, flailing his arms. The paddler—a girl—saw him. In a dozen strokes she was beside him. She held out her paddle and Hugo clutched it.

She waited for him to catch his breath. "Why aren't you wearing a life jacket?" she said sternly. "Why didn't you stay with the boat?"

"I tried to," he protested, "but it went away from me."

"It's not deep out here," she called to Tim and me. "I can see bottom." She turned back to Hugo. "Are you sure you can't touch?"

He shook his head. "P-p-pull me in."

"Can't," said the girl. "Sorry. I'd tip. And I can't tow you in, because you're holding on to my paddle."

"I'll swim out and get him," Tim shouted.

"No, you won't!" I said.

Just then Hugo called out, "Hey, my foot's on a rock."

"Well, that makes things a whole lot simpler," said the girl. "You wade in and I'll get your boat. Go on," she coaxed him. "You can do it."

Finally Hugo let go of the paddle. He floundered in toward the shallow water and staggered to shore. His lips were blue, and his teeth were chattering so hard he couldn't talk.

"You better run up to the cottage and get changed right away," I said. "And try not to get caught!" He scuttled past me up the path, arms stuck out, water dripping from him in sheets.

Second major crisis today. Mom wasn't going to like this one bit.

The girl was poking at the capsized boat with her paddle. "I can hardly move it. It's going to take me ages to get it to shore."

Tim had his shirt back on, but I could feel him twitching to go to the rescue. "Don't even think about it," I said.

The girl maneuvered the overturned boat so it pointed in our direction. Then she lined up her canoe behind it and dug her paddle into the water. The boat moved forward sluggishly. She dug harder. Inch by inch, she shunted the boat toward shore. Tim rolled up his pants and waded out to drag it the last bit.

The girl beached her canoe on the sand and climbed out. She was as tall as Tim, maybe taller, with broad shoulders and wildly curly red hair. She had green eyes and pale skin with freckles, not exactly pretty but friendly looking. She was wearing a red hoodie, and her jeans were wet up to her knees.

She stuck her hand out at each of us in turn, like an adult. "I'm Cass Marlan, from the next cottage over. Short for Cassandra, from Greek mythology. It means 'One who utters unheeded prophecies.' Isn't that awful? Makes you wonder what my parents were on."

Her hand was cold, wet and very strong. I tried not to wince. "I'm Leia. This is my brother, Tim."

"Leia? Like Princess Leia?"

Everybody always thought that. "No. It was my grand-mother's name."

"Cool."

I noticed her staring at Tim. "He has chicken pox," I said, in case she thought he had terminal acne.

"What next cottage?" Tim asked. "I didn't know there were any others."

Cass waved toward the point. "Over the hill. Me and my parents got here last night to open up. Want me to help you flip the boat over?"

Hugo reappeared while we were heaving on the wreck. He watched us drag it up on the beach. "Mom didn't see me," he said, looking pleased with himself. "I don't know where she went."

"For a walk—lucky for you." I pulled off my fleece sweatshirt and shoved it at him. He was a bit blue around the mouth. "Put this on. Where'd you leave your wet clothes?"

"Under the bed."

"Hugo! You'd better get them before Mom sees." She was already set to head back to the city. She'd go berserk if she found out about Hugo and the lake.

Cass held up Hugo's shoes and poured two streams of water from them. "You want these? I found them floating out to sea."

"What I can't figure out is how you got out there," Tim said. He turned around and looked at the boathouse. The doors were wide open, with a metal track leading down to the water. "How'd you get inside, anyway? I tried. It was locked."

"I climbed in a window."

"But why'd you take the boat out? Anyone can see it's a wreck."

"I don't know about boats," Hugo huffed. "I just opened the doors and it started to roll away."

26

"Sure, all by itself."

"He said he didn't mean to, Tim," I said. "He's only eight."

Hugo squeezed more water out of his shoes. "I pushed it a bit," he admitted. "I didn't think it would go anywhere. It started getting away, so I had to jump in."

"It's not his fault it sank," said Cass. "The people who used to own the place totally didn't look after things."

"And the water was deep, right over my head," Hugo went on. "I can't swim in this lake, Leia, not like at the Y."

"You could have drowned." Water was still dripping down his neck from his hair. I tried to wipe it away, but he shrugged me off.

"He's been sick," I told Cass. "They both had very bad cases of chicken pox. Hugo could get pneumonia."

"I thought only little kids got chicken pox."

Tim glared at her. "Anybody can get it."

"You can die of it," I said.

Hugo was kicking at the boat, not paying attention. "There's a hole in the bottom. No wonder it leaked."

"That's not where it leaked," Tim said. "That's the centerboard case."

"You know about boats," said Cass.

"A bit. At sailing camp we had Nutshells, sort of like this." He picked at the peeling paint. "Too bad it's all rotten."

"It's not that bad," said Cass. "We've got its mate. My grandfather had them built. The wood should be okay." She pointed at the back. "That's why it sank. The drain plug is out."

"What dumb person did that?" Hugo was outraged. "I could have drowned."

Tim looked thoughtful. "Maybe we could fix it up."

"Strip it and varnish it, like ours," Cass suggested.

Hugo was scrambling up the boathouse ramp. "I can see paint in here," he called out.

The boathouse smelled of dust and oil, and everything was draped in spiderwebs. The shelves were a jumble of boxes and crumpled paper bags. There were paint cans, too, and Tim found an old screwdriver and started opening them. They were all different colors: yellow and red and blue. None of them looked right for a boat. "You could do the floorboards," said Cass. "If you mix enough colors, you always get brown."

"Where's a brush?" Hugo was keen to start right away.

But Tim said it had to be scraped down and caulked first. "Anyway, it needs to dry out."

Cass grinned at Hugo. "Don't you hate people who always do things properly?"

"We could ask Mom for advice," I said. "She's a painter."

"Yeah?" Cass looked interested. "Houses or pictures?"

"Pictures. Her name's Rose Greenway. She's a bit famous, at least in Toronto." Cass didn't react like she'd heard of her, though. I tried to explain what Mom painted. "Old stuff. Doorknobs and blenders, rusty exhaust pipes." It sounded kind of crazy, but we'd started to think that dragging junk home for her was just normal. And other people seemed to think her painting was really good.

Cass was walking around, picking up things and poking in corners. She held up a lumpy gray object. "Hey, cool, a prehistoric life jacket. You should clear out this stuff and put up hammocks and sleep down here. You'd have to plug the cracks to keep out the mosquitoes, though." She slapped at one on her cheek, leaving a bright splash of blood. "Omigod, I hope it didn't have West Nile." She looked from Hugo to Tim. "I'm as healthy as a horse, but you sick guys better watch it."

Just then a strange sound came from somewhere close by. We looked around, alarmed. It rose and fell, somewhere between a screech and a low laugh. "What *is* that?"

"A loon?" Tim guessed.

We heard it again. "That's not a dying bird, that's Dad calling me," said Cass, jumping off the boathouse ramp onto the shore. "He does wolf howls better. It means I gotta go help with supper. See you later." She pushed her canoe into the water and jumped aboard.

"She seems nice," I said after Cass and her canoe had disappeared around the point. "I hope she's going to be here this summer."

"What's her name again?" Hugo asked.

"Cass."

"Yeah, Cass. She's okay, but bossy."

"She saved your life," I reminded Hugo.

"She's good in an emergency," Tim agreed. "But she *is* kind of bossy."

Three

—————————— ➤ ——————————

I HEARD LOONS CALLING IN THE NIGHT—real ones, not Cass's dad. There was a big difference. In the morning, more birds woke me when it was hardly light. They were making a worse racket with their singing and chirping than the traffic at home, but I didn't mind. I could just lie in bed looking out the window at the brightening sky, not a worry in my head except how I was going to have the most possible fun all day. When I got too excited to lie there any longer, I got up and put on my clothes.

I tiptoed to the bathroom and then checked the boys' room. Hugo was all rolled up in his blankets in the top bunk. Rover was in her cage in the corner, cleaning her ears.

Tim's bunk was empty.

Grabbing my jacket, I smeared myself with bug repellant, then eased out the door so the catch wouldn't clunk and wake Mom. I figured Tim would be down at the boathouse. I was right. Once Tim gets an idea in his head, he won't let go until it's finished. He's like our old cat Smokey that way—when Smokey knew there was a chipmunk hiding under a rock, you could bring her in the house, pat her and put food in front of her, but she'd still be thinking "chipmunk, chipmunk, chipmunk" for the rest of the day. Tim's the same way.

The boat was already up on wooden boxes and Tim was busy scraping off the peeling paint. But the surprising part wasn't that he had gotten started so fast—it was that the girl from the next cottage was there, too.

"You guys are up early," I said.

Cass grinned at me. "I was going by in my canoe, and there was Tim. The paint comes off like magic. 'Course, it was half off to begin with."

They'd already cleared a big section down to bare wood. "Somebody painted over varnish," Tim said. "No wonder it didn't stick." His scraper lifted off a strip of paint a foot long.

"It looks fun."

Cass passed me her scraper. "You can take a turn, if you want. My hand's stiff." She straightened up, rubbed her back and walked out on the dock. The lake was steaming in the sun, and the moisture frizzed her hair into red-gold corkscrews.

A duck hurtled past our heads like a missile, quacking its head off. It was so low I could hear its wings squeaking. It startled me and I jumped. Cass laughed. "Looks like it's trying to catch a bus. Did you hear those loons last night? They were really working up to something. There's one pair that nests down the shore from us every year."

Scraping wasn't as much fun as I thought. It was hard work, actually. Sometimes you got a nice long strip, but mostly you had to fight for every inch. Tim was much better at it than me. He was going at it pretty hard. Too hard, maybe. His face was pale and sweaty between his spots.

"You don't look too good," Cass said.

"You should have seen him a week ago," I told her.

"I mean, he's sort of green. You aren't going to pass out, are you?" she asked him.

Tim put down his scraper carefully and glared at us. "I think I'll go up to the cottage for a while."

We watched him trudge up the hill. "See you," Cass called after him. "He's the oldest, right?" she said to me.

"Yeah, fifteen." I felt a bit shy talking to her on my

own, but she was so friendly I got over it almost right away.

"You like having brothers?" she asked.

"I guess so." Most kids I knew didn't seem to like their brothers and sisters much, but we got on okay most of the time. I couldn't imagine life without Hugo and Tim.

"I'm an only," she said. "I like it that way. But maybe a little brother would be okay. I don't know about a big one, though. Does Tim try to tell you what to do?"

"Not too much. Specially lately, since he's been sick."

"Poor guy. But at least it got you out of school early. I totally loathe the idea of going back to Montreal for four more weeks. But Dad has this weird idea that high school's, you know, worthwhile."

"Tim's in high school," I told her. "I'll be going into grade eight. I'm thirteen. I bet you're older."

"Fourteen. I liked thirteen better."

I found that hard to believe. "I don't think it's all that great, being a teenager. Everybody says you're not a kid anymore, but they don't treat you like an adult either."

"I hate the word 'teenager,'" Cass agreed. She dipped her feet gingerly in the water, giving little *yikes* as her toes broke the surface. "There are some advantages, though. I wasn't ever allowed to take the boat out of sight until I was thirteen. Now that I've got my senior swimming badge, I can go anywhere on the lake. At least, as long as I follow lake rules."

"Lake rules?"

Cass counted them off on her fingers. "Wear a life jacket. Take a bailing can and a flashlight and a floating rope. And a whistle. Wear sunblock at all times. No standing up in a boat. My mom's got a whole list. Anyway, just Dad and me'll be up here by ourselves most of the summer, 'cause Mom has to work. But Dad's cool about most things. How about your father?"

"He's okay, too, but we don't live with him. He and Mom got divorced." I still wasn't used to saying it, even though it happened two years ago.

"That sucks."

"It's not that bad." Half the kids I knew had one different parent from when they started out. Still, you never thought it was going to happen to you. At least Mom and Dad got along okay, and we got to spend time with Dad every holiday, which was almost as much as before they broke up. Dad traveled an awful lot with his work. I guess that was part of the problem.

"We live in Toronto now," I told her. "We used to live in Port Hope." After my parents decided to call it quits, Mom moved us to Toronto. It made sense for her painting career, I guess. If we hadn't moved, she wouldn't have been able to sell her work and we wouldn't have had enough money. Things would have been a lot worse for Dad then.

"Do you hate living in the city?"

"It's okay."

"No, it's not," said Cass, looking at me closely. "You're just making the best of it. You miss your house, right?"

My eyes filled up. How did she know? I wasn't homesick all the time. I mostly missed the maple tree outside my room and the friends I'd walked to school with since kindergarten. I missed Gran living on the next block, and I missed our family the way it was. It wouldn't have been so bad if we could have gone and lived with Gran, but she broke her hip and had to go into a retirement home. She said everybody was very nice there, but I knew she missed her own house. I sure did.

Cass was waiting for me to say something, so I gulped and went on. "I don't *hate* living in the city. It's awfully noisy, though, and dirty. I didn't used to have allergies

33

before we moved, but now I can't have a cat anymore. I'm not having allergies here so far—except my bites are swelling up a bit. But that's because I scratch them till they bleed." I stopped. I hardly knew Cass, and here I was going on and on about myself.

"Put boiling water on them," she said.

I stared at her.

"On the bites. Stops the itching."

"But wouldn't you burn yourself?"

She laughed. "Don't pour it straight out of the kettle, you idiot. Dab it on with a washcloth. Too bad about your cat," she added.

"Smokey's okay," I said. "She lives with Dad, so I get to see her when we visit. She wouldn't be happy in an apartment anyway. She's an outside cat."

"I'm an outside person." Cass went back to moaning about having to go home to Montreal. I stretched out on the dock in the sun and thought about how great it was not to have to go anywhere. I was so happy being here, listening to her talk. She was smart, nice and funny. Easy to be around. *A friend*, I thought. I'll have a real friend again. It could be a great summer.

Exactly one second later the spell was broken. A boat zoomed around the point with a roar as loud as a jet plane. It was the first big one I'd seen since we got here, bright yellow and black. It came in close before heading back out toward open water. The guy driving it waved. I waved back. Moments later the wake slapped against the dock. Cass and I scrambled out of the way, but we still got soaked.

Cass wiped the spray off her face, glowering in disgust. "They're making a lot of noise so early in the morning. Wonder where they came from?" She shaded her eyes with her hand and stared into the distance, watching the boat disappear. "I used to know all the boats on this part of the lake, but last year some new cottages went up. The people who live in them act like they own the place. Dad even heard a rumor about a trailer park! Can you imagine—on our lake! That drives me crazy. It would ruin everything! Anyway, who'd come to it? It's so far away from everything. They'd have to drive an hour even to get pizza."

"Isn't it lonely sometimes, being here all on your own?"

"I'm not usually on my own. Usually, my friend Amy comes—since we were really young, like eight or nine. She's not coming this summer, though. She's going to Vancouver to visit her cousins."

Cass sounded a little upset about it.

"Are you and Amy still friends?"

"Yeah, but..." She didn't finish the sentence.

"I bet Vancouver is fantastic. Wouldn't you go, if you could?"

"I guess so," Cass said without enthusiasm. "But not in the *summer*. You wait all winter for it finally to get warm, and then you go to Vancouver? It's a city. I don't get it. I want to be *here*. We've been coming here for a hundred years. Well, not me personally, but my great-grandfather."

Cass said our cottage used to be owned by her uncle, but he sold it and moved to the States a long time ago. "So now there's us and you on this bay, and a couple of farms and a village on the main part of the lake. And a few other cottages that have been here for a while. One belongs to the Bonnycastles. They're obscenely rich and the kids never go outside. They're like mushrooms. They watch movies and play Nintendo."

"Nintendo?" Hugo appeared around the corner of the boathouse. He was still in his Incredible Hulk boxers, his hair falling in dark wings over his sleep-creased face.

35

"XStation, Playbox, whatever," Cass said.

He stared at her suspiciously. "Xbox and PlayStation. How come you don't know that?"

"Because I don't care. And they've got satellite TV, of course. Roger and Anne-Sophie—those are their names. She's, like, seven, and Roger's ten, maybe. They don't like boats or swimming or anything interesting. But my dad sort of knows their dad because they both teach at university. So I get invited over."

"Do they let you play Nintendo?" Hugo asked.

"I don't know how and I don't want to," she retorted. Hugo stared at her like she was from another planet. "But they do have these great microscopes and telescopes and books that they don't even use. And a fantastic collection of native artifacts—really awesome. Mr. Bonnycastle's a historian. Why he married Mrs. Bonnycastle is a great mystery."

"What do you mean?" I asked.

Cass shrugged. "She's, you know, got artificial eyebrows or something. A total fake. But *he's* all right. He thinks this bay should be kept the way it is, with no more cottages, because it has so much native history. I agree, which is why a trailer park would totally suck!" She pointed across the water with her foot. "There used to be a big Indian camp over there. Around the point in Half Moon Bay. Me and Dad and Amy went to see if we could find it once."

"Iroquois?" I asked eagerly. "I did an independent study at school on native people."

"She's still mad 'cause she didn't get the best mark in the class," said Hugo.

It was true. It did bother me. I spent hours and hours in the library and carried home tons of books. Everybody else just downloaded stuff.

"It was really good," Hugo said. "She had Indian maps and everything."

"It wasn't the Iroquois over there, it was Algonkins," Cass said. "Spelled with a *k*. The Iroquois were their enemies. In my opinion, the Algonkins were better." She folded her arms, which were covered in little golden freckles. "All you hear about the Iroquois is their government and how they had these council meetings that went on and on. As bad as ancient Romans, if you ask me. Or parliament."

"They were great warriors," I said. "And farmers. They grew corn and squash and beans and watermelons."

"The Algonkins just wandered around where there was good hunting and didn't disturb the environment," Cass countered. "Everything was fine until the white people came and wrecked their hunting grounds and everything. As usual."

I suddenly remembered the flash I'd had standing at the door of the cottage. "Did Indians live on this side? On our point?"

"Why not? We picked this spot for cottages, so they probably thought it was a good place, too. But I only know for sure about them being on Half Moon Bay. You guys want to go over there and search for relics this summer? Now that I'm fourteen, I can take the boats anywhere. You want to come?"

"We'd *love* to." I hadn't even bothered to look at Hugo.

A friend and an adventure. The summer was definitely off to a good start.

Four

———————— ❧ ————————

CASS AND HER PARENTS—Naomi and Jonathan—stopped in to say goodbye on their way back to Montreal that afternoon. Naomi was tall like Cass, with curly hair. It was gray now, but it could have been red once. Cass's father was big and bald with a black beard.

When they asked how we were settling in, Mom told them all about the studio disaster. Naomi asked her who the carpenters were.

"Matt Hogan and Leonard Mitchell. I got their names from a card in the general store. Now they're not even answering the phone."

Jonathan nodded. "I know that pair. They're harmless, but lazy as spotted dogs. I hope you didn't pay them in advance."

"Some," Mom admitted.

"They'll be back when the money's gone."

"Tim might be able to fix it if they don't come back," I said.

"Yeah, Tim can do stuff," Cass told her parents. "He's fixing up their sailboat."

"Good for you," Cass's dad said, looking at Tim. "We have the twin of yours. Classic cedar-strip construction. Are you a sailor?"

"I've sailed some. Mostly on Lake Ontario."

"You'll love it here. Tricky winds and challenging. You like boats?" Obviously Jonathan Marlan did.

Naomi consulted her watch. "I know no one wants to leave, but we need to get moving, gang."

We all walked up the path with them to their drive-way, which was just over the hill. Beyond it was their cottage, which looked exactly like ours, only not so over-grown. Cass pulled a piece of paper from her pocket. "Here's our address and phone number if you want advice about your boat or anything. I hardly know you, but I miss you already." She threw her arms around me and then Hugo. She was about to do the same to Tim, but he took a step back. He wasn't about to let that happen.

Cass's father caught her by the elbow and propelled her toward the van. "Goodbye-e-e-e!" she cried as he bundled her inside. She leaned out the window and waved until they were out of sight.

"Now what?" said Hugo gloomily, scuffing the ground with his runner. "No TV, no games, no one to play with."

"You can spend some quality time with Rover," said Mom. "You've hardly looked at that poor rabbit since you got here." We headed back to our cottage, and Hugo and I followed Tim down to the boathouse. While he put away his scraping tools, I took another look around at the junk on the shelves. There was a birch-bark lamp with a chewed cord, and an old record player that played actual records—the kind with the big holes in the middle. Hugo found a picture of Queen Elizabeth when she still had brown hair.

The shelves gave me an idea. "Hey, Tim, we could move some of these up to Mom's studio for her."

"I see something," said Hugo, pointing through the cobwebs into the rafters. We all looked up. Stuck in among a bunch of oars and paddles was a long, dusty roll of cloth.

"Must be an old sail," said Tim.

"Or a rug," I said.

Hugo's eyes gleamed. "Let's get it down! Get it down!"

39

"What for?" Tim asked.

"It could be for Mom's studio!"

"It's probably all spidery and moldy," I objected, thinking of all the eight-legged creatures that might have built their homes inside.

But Hugo wouldn't let up. He got Tim to climb on a chair to drag the thing down, and we carried it outside. It was a rug. Once it had probably been red and blue and black, but the red had faded to a pinky color. It was actually sort of nice—not too moldy-smelling after all, and the spiders soon hurried on their way.

"Will it fit?" Hugo asked.

"Mom's studio, you mean? Only one way to find out." Tim rolled it up again.

The rug was heavy, but the three of us managed to drag it up the hill. We set it down on the grass, and I opened the door of Mom's studio. The coast was clear. "Careful where you step, Hugo," I said. "This floor's got a life of its own."

"Yeah, it bends when you walk on it. That's why the carpet will be good," said Hugo.

We took the loose lumber outside and dragged the rug in. Spread out, it covered most of the floor one way and all but a few feet the other. Pulling on the corners, we got it fairly straight. I swept the wrinkles out with the broom.

Hugo was so excited he was jumping up and down. "Can I get Mom and show her?"

In a few minutes he was back, pulling Mom by the hand. She stepped cautiously inside and gazed around in bewilderment. "Who *did* all this?"

"We did! Is it okay?" Hugo was making nervous faces, clenching his teeth and scowling.

"What a difference! I can hardly believe my eyes."

"I knew she'd like it! I knew she'd like it!" he crowed.

"The rug was all Hugo's idea," I said. "Tim fixed the window. I'm going to wash it for you. And we found some shelves, too."

"Oh, you guys. It's fantastic," Mom said, her eyes filling with tears. "It'll have to be made weather-tight, but I can work in it for now. I didn't think I'd be able to. I've been feeling just sick about it. I've called and called those men, and they never answer. I shouldn't have given them so much money."

As if on cue, the sound of a vehicle crunching up our laneway drifted through the open door. It was sort of uncanny. "Somebody's just driven in, Mom," said Tim, sticking his head out to listen. "It's a truck."

"That's them," Mom said grimly. "My carpenters."

I heard doors slam. A minute later I saw two men in baseball caps and team jackets come trudging up the path. Mom folded her arms across her chest. "How ya doing?" the bigger guy called out.

They clomped in the door. Hands shoved in their pockets, they rocked back and forth in their heavy boots, looking around, looking at us. They took up a lot of space.

"We didn't get it quite done," the bigger one said. I tried not to stare at his hairy stomach bulging over his jeans. It wasn't a fashion statement—at least not one that anybody would want to make.

"Me and Lenny finished fixin' your roof and the floor, but we ran out of money for the rest." He grinned at Mom. With her short, spiky hair and young-looking face, he probably figured she'd be a pushover.

She wasn't. "I gave you $700 for supplies," she snapped. "You said that would be plenty."

The big one—he must be Matt—pushed his cap back on his head. "Yeah, I know, but the lumber cost more than we thought." He was still grinning, like a big Lab.

41

"An' it took a lot longer than we figured, too. It's kind of a tricky job, eh?"

"You told me it was a simple one." Mom's expression made it clear she was *not* happy. "Replace some shingles and rotten floorboards. Cut a window, put up a workbench and shelves. That's what we agreed on. Fifteen hundred total." She pointed to the window. "That wasn't even safe until my son fixed it. You could see daylight around the edges."

Matt shifted from one foot to another. His voice got louder. "Like I said, lady, it's not done, only the roof and the floor. Me and Lenny can do the rest for you—but it'll cost more."

"No." Mom's lips were a thin line. "We agreed on a price, $1,500. And I'm not even prepared to pay you that. The work you did is appalling. You didn't do what you promised. Are you really even carpenters at all?"

"Now hold on one minute." Matt's big smile was gone, and now his arms were folded, too. "I figure you're takin' advantage. You come up here from the city an' think you can treat us like a bunch of hicks? Cheat us out of what you owe us?"

He and Mom argued back and forth. This was *not* good, and a glance at Tim made it even worse. His face was going red and I could see him clenching his hands, dying to defend Mom. But getting into a fight didn't seem like the best option. Even the skinny guy looked like he could probably flatten Tim, and Matt could probably do some real damage. And what if they had guns in their truck? Now that Cass's family had gone, there was nobody around for miles.

"Mr. Marlan next door says you're good guys," I blurted out. They looked at me, then at each other. I just wanted them to know we'd been talking about them—

that they couldn't kill us and dump our bodies and think nobody would ever connect them to the crime.

Meanwhile, Mom had taken out her wallet. She scribbled some figures on a check and ripped it out. Matt took it and peered at it suspiciously. "Three hundred? That ain't enough." He tossed it back at her. "That's not what we agreed on."

She let the piece of paper flutter to the floor. "I already gave you what you said you needed for supplies. I don't believe you spent half of it. A thousand dollars for what you've done is generous, and you know it. Somebody else is going to have to fix your mess."

Matt's face reddened and he seemed to swell up even bigger. "Oh, yeah, lady? That ain't—"

"C'mon, Matt, let's get going." The other one, Lenny, bent and snatched up the check. Shaking the sawdust off, he headed out the door.

Matt stood his ground a little longer. Then he followed his buddy. "Damn city smart-asses," he muttered over his shoulder. He said some other things, too.

We listened in silence until we heard the engine start. The truck roared and sputtered back out to the road. The noise faded into the distance.

Hugo and I put our arms around Mom. Tim patted her shoulder. "You were really brave," he told her. "Standing up to them like that."

"My knees were quaking," she said. "But I couldn't stand being taken advantage of."

I felt shaky all over. For sure she wouldn't want to stay now, not after this. Why couldn't *anything* go right? Everything was supposed to be better now that we were here. I felt a rush of anger toward Dad. If he'd been here, none of this would have happened. Those guys wouldn't have acted like that with Dad.

43

"But we're not going to let this get to us," said Mom. "Those guys are dealt with, and, thanks to you, I can start to work."

"Then you're not going to take us home?" I asked.

"No. Where did you ever get that idea, you funny girl?"

Suddenly, I felt a whole lot better.

Five

---➤---

"WHAT'S A SABBATICAL?" Hugo asked while we were chopping vegetables for the pasta. He slipped Rover some parsley. "Is it better than being a consultant, like Dad?"

"What?" I wiped tomato on my nose. "I don't get you."

"A sabbatical. What Cass said Mr. Marlan is."

"Jonathan Marlan isn't *a* sabbatical, Hugo," said Mom. "He's *on* sabbatical. It means he has time off from his university teaching. He's writing a book on politics."

"Uck."

"I'm sure he finds it more interesting than you do."

"I got a chicken pox sabbatical," Hugo said smugly.

I set the table for supper. Every plate in the cupboard was different, and we all had favorites picked out already. Mine was a blue willow pattern with birds and Chinese people. Mom's had fruit on it, and Tim's had blue stripes. Hugo picked an old Bunnykins plate with a rabbit in a dunce cap in the middle and running rabbits around the edge. Tim said it was a kid's dish, but Hugo didn't care.

For dessert we had fresh fruit salad with ice cream. Mom drank her tea and wrote a letter on her laptop. When she was finished, she got up to get a sweater. "It's chilly enough tonight to get the fireplace going, don't you think? There's a bag of marshmallows in the cupboard. All we need is wood."

Tim was lying on the sofa reading old yachting magazines. All of the scraping had worn him out. Hugo and I went out to the woodpile. The sun had set, and twilight was taking all the color out of everything. Hugo was right on my heels. "I don't like the dark."

"It's not dark, only dusk." I piled his arms with logs. The moon was coming up big and yellow over the lake, and I got a sudden urge to go down to the water. "Take these in and help Mom get the fire going. I'll bring more in a minute."

"Where are you going?" he asked indignantly.

"Just to sit on the dock."

"What if I want to come?"

"You don't." I ran down the boathouse path, pulling up my hood against the mosquitoes.

"What if something grabs me?" he wailed after me.

Night was coming on fast, and the woods looked dark and deep. Little white trillium faces glimmered from the hillside. Things rustled in the leaves near the path. I tried not to let the noises bother me. It was plain silly to imagine a leopard crouching behind a bush. I definitely didn't want to be the kind of person who was afraid of the dark.

Of course, there could be skunks. I kept my eyes on the ground, alert for a white stripe. But I met no skunks or anything else even remotely scary. I walked to the end of the dock and sat, swinging my feet over the water.

I'd always thought it would be quiet in the country, but it wasn't. The birds were settling down, except for a few stray robins, but now the frogs were starting up, high-pitched and crickety. Insects thrummed in a cloud above my head. I wondered what Cass was doing now.

A great blue ring glowed around the moon. Rain, that was supposed to mean—or was it werewolves? Patches of mist rose from the swamp at the end of the bay. Will-o'-the-wisps, Dad called them.

Across the bay on the far green shore, Cass said, Algonkins once lived. I imagined them there—tiny figures

46

like the lead ones in Tim's old set, with miniature toma-hawks and bows and arrows. I could almost see them moving by the shore. Once, long ago, they'd built homes there and made birch-bark canoes.

Something crossed the moonlight path out on the water and set it dancing. An animal? A muskrat, or beaver? No, it was bigger. I squinted into the darkness. A boat. It was a canoe, coming around the point like Cass had. But this time, it wasn't Cass.

The canoe came straight toward me. In a minute or two it would pass the dock. I sat stock-still, hugging my knees. I could hear the paddle dipping in the water, and I could make out a figure kneeling in the stern. But it was too dark to see a face.

All of a sudden a line of poetry from an old book of Gran's popped into my mind, something about a ghostly paddler: *"The Indian fixed like bronze, Trails his severed head through the dead water, holding it by the hair."*

I sat like a statue, not daring to breathe. But the pad-dler must have seen me—I was only twenty feet away. The dipping stopped. The frog chorus fell silent. Everything waited, listening.

Then, with a liquid sound, the canoe turned and headed swiftly back out toward the open lake. A moment later not even a ripple showed that anything had been there.

Dimly I became aware of someone calling my name. I began to breathe again, but my scalp still crawled with fear.

"Leia?"

It was Mom. She sounded worried. I lurched to my feet on numb legs. Something moved in the bushes, and I swerved in panic on the path and raced up the hill.

Mom was in the lighted doorway, peering out. She stepped back as I burst in. "Leia! Are you all right?"

47

"Yes. Why wouldn't I be?" My voice sounded funny, high and quavery.

"I didn't know where you'd got to. It's awfully dark for you to be out."

"I was just down on the dock. I told Hugo where I was going."

"I know, he told me. Sorry, sweetie, I'm a little paranoid after that run-in with those oafs today. You're still in time for marshmallows. Any longer and Tim and Hugo would have eaten them all."

"Where's the wood you were s'posed to bring in?" Hugo asked.

"Oh, yeah." I went out again and gathered a hasty armload.

Mom held the door for me. "Quick, before the bugs get in. Are you sure you're all right? You look like you've seen a ghost."

"I'm okay." I dumped the logs on the hearth, startling Rover who was warming herself in front of the fire. She squealed and leapt in the air, nearly scaring me out of my skin again. I swallowed a shriek as she zigzagged away to safer territory. "Sorry! Poor bunny!"

"You nearly clobbered her." Hugo held a blackened lump under my nose.

"I apologized." My heartbeat returned to normal. "What's that supposed to be?"

"A perfect marshmallow."

"It's pure carbon, Hugo."

"I like carbon."

I knelt in front of the fire, chewing a raw marshmallow while I waited for the one on my fork to get brown. In the heart of the fire, tiny blue flames licked the darkness. If I stared hard enough, I could see a tiny paddler on their gleaming path. What *was* that out on the bay? Had I really seen something, or was I imagining things again? Probably it was only somebody out for an evening paddle.

It couldn't have been an Indian, after all. No Indians lived around here anymore, Mom said. I decided to keep it to myself, the same as yesterday when I looked through the windows of the cottage at the lake. Tim and Hugo would say I was crazy.

Six

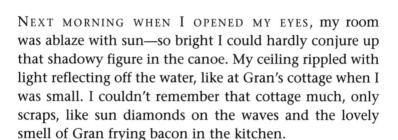

NEXT MORNING WHEN I OPENED MY EYES, my room was ablaze with sun—so bright I could hardly conjure up that shadowy figure in the canoe. My ceiling rippled with light reflecting off the water, like at Gran's cottage when I was small. I couldn't remember that cottage much, only scraps, like sun diamonds on the waves and the lovely smell of Gran frying bacon in the kitchen.

I stretched my feet to the bottom of the bed, thinking of all the wonderful things I was going to do today. First: Eat as much cracked-wheat toast with peanut butter and grape jelly as I wanted. Second: Choose a book from my stack and take it down to the dock to read. I'd brought all my Narnia books—which I'd had since I was six—and a lovely one that used to be Gran's, called *A Girl of the Limberlost*. I read them again every summer. And I had a stack of new ones, too, bought with my birthday bookstore gift certificates. I'd been saving them until we got here.

I threw back the covers and stepped out of my pajamas. The bureau mirror had blotches and clouds in it, like it was worn out from reflecting too many people. My pale face and skinny arms and tiny little breasts glimmered fish-flesh white.

Third on the list: Get a tan.

In the kitchen Hugo was eating cereal and squeaking like some Japanese cartoon character. Mom was sorting seeds. While I was waiting for my toast, I picked up a couple of packages. "Red Marvel Carrots. Rocket Radishes.

Webb's Wonder Lettuce. Whose garden is this going to be, Mom? Rover's?"

"I thought you kids needed a project. Hugo's having TV withdrawal."

"Am not," Hugo grumbled. "I got my Game Boy. S'only got four games, though."

"Why do I need a project?" I asked. "I've got my whole day planned. What about Tim?"

"Tim's supposed to be taking it easy."

"He's got a funny way of doing that. I bet he's already down at the boathouse."

Mom nodded. "Just like his father." Then she smiled so I wouldn't think she was criticizing Dad. Ever since the split she and Dad were careful not to say mean things about each other in front of us.

"Well, *I'm* not planting any arugula."

After breakfast, Mom led us to a spot behind the wood-pile. Two shovels leaned against a tree. She pointed to a big space that she'd already cleared of sumac. "I've got a feeling this is the perfect place for a garden. It gets lots of sun and there's plenty of earth."

I took a shovel and muttered, "I bet Cass's dad doesn't make her do hard labor."

But except for tree roots, the sandy soil was easy to dig, and the breeze off the lake blew most of the blackflies away. The hardest part of the job was listening to Hugo moan. He was missing some stupid program about psychic iguanas. Every now and then he stopped moaning long enough to put worms in a plastic container. "I'm saving them to fish with."

"Don't take them all. Gardens need worms."

"Fish need them, too. When can we stop? I'm boiling."

I pulled off my sweatshirt. "We're not even halfway finished. You couldn't bury anybody in what we've done so far. Mom said we have to dig to the trees."

"What's she going to grow in here anyway? Hay?" Hugo squatted to grab another worm. Then he leaned down for a closer look. "Hey, Leia."

"What?"

He picked something up. "I found a pen."

I went over and peered at the dirt-smeared object. It was a fountain pen, black with a metal nib that somebody must have stepped on. "Too bad it's broken."

"I might be able to fix it. Finders keepers." He went back to digging with new enthusiasm. "Maybe I'll find something else." In the next little while he turned up a small blue bottle and a greenish one with the top broken off. Then a yellow cup with no handle.

My side of the garden had nothing but worms, so I went over to Hugo's side. Soon my shovel clanked on something. I loosened it.

A rock. I heaved it into the bushes in disgust. "Hugo, you're finding all the good stuff. Let me dig where you are."

But he wouldn't budge. He'd found what looked like a petrified loaf of bread—at least we couldn't think of anything else it might be. It was gray and oblong and seemed to be made of stuck-together slices. Weird.

Finally my shovel hit something else. "Another lousy rock, I bet." I scraped away at it. What I'd uncovered was flat and hard. Were those cracks in it, or some sort of design? Maybe it wasn't a rock after all.

"It could be a giant trilobite," Hugo said hopefully.

I pried the thing out of the ground. It was about the size of my hand and slightly curved. A piece of broken pottery! "I'm taking it down to the lake to wash it," I told Hugo. I hurried down the path to the dock with Hugo close behind me. Bending down, I dunked my discovery in the water, scrubbing away the mud.

52

Tim stopped scraping the boat and came over. "What have you got?"

"A piece of pottery, I think. It could be native."

"Don't rub so hard. You'll break it," he said.

There was definitely a pattern scratched into the rust-colored clay surface. I sat back on my heels. "It's Indian. I'm sure of it."

"Indian!" Hugo hooted. "Let's go back and dig. Maybe there's more stuff!"

We raced back to the garden. A little while after, I uncovered a speckled tin plate with a hole rusted through it. "That's not Indian, though," I said to Hugo. It must have been the excitement of my discovery, or maybe it was working in the sun for too long, but I made a bit of a mistake: I told Hugo about the ghostly paddler from the night before.

Hugo's eyes grew wide. "A real ghost?"

"I don't know. Maybe. Don't tell Tim," I added.

Right then Tim came up from the boathouse. "Any more shovels?" he asked.

"I saw one under the cottage," I said, and he went to get it. We all dug for another twenty minutes or so, but the only thing that turned up was another old glass bottle that Hugo—of course—found.

"You find anything, Tim?" I asked. He'd started on another patch at the edge of the sumacs.

"Nope."

I stopped. "That must've been the only—"

Just then my shovel clunked on something. It came out quite easily—another piece of pottery, slightly smaller than the first. When I washed it, I could see that the design was a bit different.

Mom came to check on our progress and couldn't believe how much we'd dug. Hugo and I showed her our finds.

"This must have been the rubbish dump when the cottage was first built," she said.

"What about these?" I pointed at the pottery pieces. "They're not garbage. I'm sure they're native. I've seen pictures."

Mom turned the fragments over. "They could be, I guess. I don't know anything about Indian ceramics, but I certainly don't see 'Made in China' on the back." She began raking the soil we'd dug and added some bits of glass to our collection. Hugo was overjoyed to find the top of his fountain pen.

Then, the patch where Tim was digging turned up something new: bones. One was about six inches long and as big around as Hugo's wrist. There were smaller, broken bits as well.

"They might be human," Hugo said excitedly.

"Yeah. The big one might be a leg bone with the end chewed off," Tim said, his voice dripping with sarcasm.

"Maybe this is a cemetery." Hugo sounded worried now.

"Don't pay any attention to Tim," I said. "It's a cow bone. If it *was* a cemetery, it'd have to be one for old cups and fountain pens and Indian pottery, too."

"People used to get buried with their favorite possessions," Tim argued. "These could be the bones of an Indian writer buried with his best bowl and fountain pen. And then wolves dug him up and dragged off everything except his thigh bone. Now that we've disturbed him, he'll probably come out at night and haunt us. All scalped and chewed with his eyeballs on fire."

"Tim," Mom said warningly. "That's a soup bone."

But after supper that night Hugo wouldn't go out for

54

wood. The woodpile was too near the garden, he said. Honestly, I felt a little uneasy going myself. But the lake at twilight was so magical, alive with insects and bats and swallows swooping low over the water. The frog chorus was like a wall of sound. I crept out on the dock, my eyes fixed on the point, excitement welling in my throat. I half hoped, half dreaded that the ghost canoe would come back out of the mist and cross the moonlit path on the water.

But the moon hadn't even risen yet, and after a minute the mosquitoes discovered me. I scurried up the path, grabbed as many logs as I could carry and slipped back into the cottage.

Seven

❧

THERE WERE NO MORE GHOST SIGHTINGS in the three weeks before Cass came back. The days settled into a blissful, sunny routine. I read through the books on the living-room shelves—old Agatha Christie mysteries and some others that Mom wouldn't have approved of if she'd known about them. Tim worked on the boat. Mom got set up in her studio and started painting. And Hugo whined about how boring it was, but a couple of times Mom took him into Pembroke when she went shopping and let him get good and banged up on his skateboard. That kept him quiet for a while.

The Saturday after school ended, I kept an ear open for Cass all morning. Hugo and I were swimming some time after lunch when I finally heard a car in our laneway. "Listen, Hugo!" The car turned up the hill to the Marlans' cottage. I ran from the water, grabbed my towel and headed straight up the path with Hugo at my heels.

It was Cass all right. She burst out of the van, her hair quivering with outrage. "Hell and brimstone!"

Hugo and I stared at her with our mouths hanging open.

"You haven't seen it?"

"Seen what?" I asked.

"Right at *our* gate." The freckles stood out on her livid face. "Across from *our* mailbox. The ugliest, tackiest sign *ever*! Billboard, actually. It's that huge."

Her father opened the back of the van and began unloading bags onto the grass. "Advertising Pelletier's," he explained. "The general store in the village."

56

"No."

"So, when are you going to finish that boat?"

"It's getting there."

"What are you going to name it? Ours is called *Arrow*."

"Ours could be *Bow*," Hugo said.

"How about *Disaster*, after your maiden voyage," Cass suggested.

"Or what about *Rover*?" said Hugo.

"That's the name of his rabbit," I told Cass.

"Because I wish I had a dog and Mom never lets me get one."

Cass thought about it. "*Rover*'s not bad, but we need something a little more nautical. What about *White Water*? Or *Seagull*?"

"It's not white," Tim said impatiently, "and this isn't the sea."

"What about just *Gull*?" I said. "They're brown when they're young and learning to fly, and we're just starting to sail. Me and Hugo, anyway."

Hugo liked it. Tim shrugged. *Gull* it was.

Cass wanted to know what we'd been doing all the time she was in Montreal. "Swimming and reading and eating," I said. We'd gone with Mom into the village to shop and driven to Pembroke a couple of times. We'd also painted nearly every room in the cottage. I tried to think of what else.

Hugo prodded me. "Remember what you have to show her, Leia? What we found—you know—in the garden."

How could I have forgotten! I flew up the path. The box was under my bed. I grabbed it and was out the door before Mom could tell me off for tracking in sand.

I handed the box to Cass. Inside were the two pieces of pottery, wrapped in cloth. I'd scrubbed them clean, but you could see where one had been blackened by fire. Cass picked them up carefully. "Wow, these must be really old. Where did you find them?"

"In our garden. At least, it's a garden now. It used to be a dump. I think they're native."

"For sure they are," said Cass. "We should dig for more."

"We did. That's all there was," said Tim.

"It was weird we found pottery in with all the old garbage," I said. "Do you think it might have been here already? I mean, before the cottage was built?"

Cass ran her finger over the designs in the clay. "Maybe. I only know for sure about the camp at Half Moon Bay."

"We're going over there to hunt for relics, right?" I reminded her. "You said."

"Yeah." She stood up. "How about after lunch?"

Tim didn't want to come, but Hugo and I went in Cass's canoe. It was straight across the bay, less than a mile. With three of us paddling, it didn't take too long.

We pulled the canoe up on shore and tied it to a tree. Hugo gazed around, puzzled. The trees came right down to the waterline. "I don't see anything. Where's the Indian camp?"

Cass pointed into the woods. "About half a mile that way. You can't get near it by water. Too marshy." She plunged into the trees. The ground was rocky and steeply sloped. "Stay together, okay? We don't want anybody getting lost."

I couldn't see a path, but Cass seemed to know where she was going. Hugo and I followed her through birches and cedars, ducking under branches and trying to watch for poison ivy. After that the hill leveled off and we got into a pine forest. The going was much easier on the carpet of fallen needles.

60

Bands of sunlight filtered through the waving treetops and rippled on the ground like live things. "Everything's stripey," said Hugo. "Hey, good camouflage. Specially if you were a tiger."

"Or a wolf," I added.

"There are no wolves around here, are there?" he asked Cass uneasily.

"Never seen any. Could be bears, but they mostly hang around the dump. We hear coyotes, and I guess there are wolves in the winter. Pelletier—the one with the sign—told us a story once, about a couple of guys hunting near here in the fall. They blew their moose horns and a wolf pack answered. They ran all the way back to their truck and jumped inside, and the wolves followed them. If they hadn't got to their truck, they would have been lunch."

"Why didn't they shoot them with their guns?" asked Hugo.

"Well, maybe there were too many wolves to shoot. I don't remember."

It didn't sound right to me. "There are no confirmed reports of wolves attacking people. They only attack small animals or sick or wounded ones. Farley Mowat says most things you hear about wolves are just rumors and lies."

Cass raised her eyebrows. "Oh, yeah? If we meet any, you be sure to tell them that, okay?"

We talked about wolves until the pines ended and we entered a clearing. A flock of yellow birds burst out of a tangle of raspberry bushes and flew up into the trees. Hugo grabbed my shirt. "Look, Leia!" he whispered.

On the far side of the glade stood a deer, gazing back at us. It didn't have antlers like the one over our fireplace. Must be a doe. I held my breath. We stood perfectly still, but after a minute she flicked her ears and walked away.

Then, with a bound and a white flash of tail, she was gone. It was magical.

"That was cool," Cass grinned. "You don't see deer much at this time of day." She gazed around. "I think the camp was somewhere near here."

"Does anybody own this property?" I didn't want to get into trouble for trespassing.

Cass wasn't sure. "Dad and I went to the record office in Pembroke once to figure out who owns what around the lake. I think this might be Crown land. Some of it belongs to farmers, and somebody named Cameron or Campbell owns some. And the Bonnycastles—remember I told you about them? They own some of it, too. Anyway, nobody would mind us being here."

"What are we supposed to be looking for?" Hugo asked.

"Arrowheads, I guess. Things like that. I guess the Algonkins wouldn't have had house foundations, right? So just any sign of human habitation."

We spread out. I poked with a stick at the earth wherever it showed through the weeds. Hugo was flailing at the horseflies and kicking raspberry canes. He came over and showed me where one had scratched him and left a track of tiny beads of blood along his arm. "There's nothing here," he said grumpily. "When are we going home?"

"We've only just started, Hugo. Look for arrowheads, why don't you?"

"I've already looked for them. What about a tomahawk?"

"Good idea." I walked quickly away from him. I wanted to be able to concentrate, to think about what it would have been like when people lived here long ago.

From my independent study project, I figured there'd have been bark-roofed houses with grassy paths between them. I tried to picture the raspberry tangle and weeds gone, the tall pines around the clearing cut down for buildings and firewood. There'd have been kids, maybe playing hide-and-seek. Grown-ups pounding corn and cutting up meat. A girl my own age with braided hair, stirring a clay pot over a fire.

I had a feeling that imagining would lead me to something, some trace. But it was hard to focus. Hugo kept talking to me and goofing around. Then, across the clearing, Cass started yelling. "Hey, guys, come here!"

She was pointing up through the woods at a rocky cliff. I stood behind her, my eyes following her finger. "There's an old shed or something up there. See?"

A mossy roof showed through the trees at the top of the ridge. "Might be an old sugaring shack," she said.

"Or an Indian cabin!" said Hugo.

We picked our way through the woods and started up the steep hillside, pulling ourselves up using branches and tree trunks. It was hard going, over and around huge rocks. When we neared the top, I could see that the building was a log cabin. But between it and us stood a strange apparition.

Hugo's eyes grew round. "That's so weird!"

Deep in the woods, miles from anywhere, a heap of junk like a giant magpie's hoard was piled around a tree stump. Somehow, the stump was still alive. Stubby branches grew from it, and a few green leaves stuck out here and there. It was hung like a Christmas tree with bits of colored plastic and shiny foil, garlanded with snarls of cassette tape.

We circled the strange sculpture uneasily—an old tire and lots of hubcaps, rusty cans strung on a wire. Somebody had shoved a Spider-man action figure inside a green plastic pop bottle. A bunch of golf balls hung in a plastic onion bag. Silver beer cans were stacked in a clementine box. Most of these things were faded and weathered, but some seemed pretty new. On the very top was a cow's skull wearing mirrored sunglasses. I was staring at it when a tiny eye peered over one of the lenses.

I shrieked and fled, with Hugo and Cass right behind me. Skidding, slipping, grabbing at trees, we tore down the hill. We got all the way back to the clearing before we stopped, panting. "What was *that*?"

"It winked at me." Hugo's voice was high and shaky.

Nobody wanted to climb the hill again for a second look.

When we got back to our dock, Hugo started telling Tim about the scary junk thing in the woods. Tim kept sanding away at the boat and not really listening—just like when Hugo tried to tell him the plot of some incredibly dumb TV show and Tim said, "Uh-huh, uh-huh," and kept on with whatever he was doing.

"It was way in the woods and there was an Indian cabin, but we didn't see any Indians. There was this cow skull on the top and it was wearing sunglasses and then it winked at us."

"Uh-huh. An Indian skull."

"No, you aren't listening, Tim!" Hugo scowled. "It was a *cow* skull and it was on this tree that had beer cans and branches coming out of it. I saw it move."

"The tree?"

"No, the skull. It winked."

"Maybe the tree moved. Like the Ents in *The Lord of the Rings*."

I could see Hugo didn't like this idea.

"Sounds like something Mom might paint," Tim said. "It was just junk, right? Not body parts?"

"Don't talk like that, Tim!" Hugo's face went red.

"It was just junk, but it creeped us right out," I said. "Who would have put it there?"

"Somebody with a bad sense of humor? Are you going back?"

Hugo shook his head emphatically.

But if we didn't go back, how were we going to find any Indian relics?

"We could try the fields over there," said Cass. She pointed off in the distance to where our bay opened onto the main part of the lake. "Dad and I found an arrowhead there once. Do you want to come, Tim?"

He shook his head.

"We could sail over tomorrow in our boat. You can sail it, if you want," she added slyly. "To see how it handles."

He thought about it. "I guess I could go, then," he said.

Eight

WE WERE ALL SET TO LEAVE the next morning, when Mom wrecked our plans. She'd been in the village shopping at Pelletier's when she ran into Mrs. Bonnycastle. "She's invited you over to meet her kids," Mom said. "I told her you'd love to."

Tim begged off, of course, claiming he was still contagious—even though he hardly had any spots left. Hugo didn't mind going, though. He remembered Cass saying that the Bonnycastles had video games. And I sort of wanted to see what their place was like.

When we went over to Cass's to tell her, it turned out Mrs. Bonnycastle had phoned up and invited her, too. "I've only just got here, Dad," she fumed, stomping around the kitchen. "I finally get out of school and have a chance to have some fun, and they spoil it. They're the last people in the world I want to hang out with right now. It's a huge drag. They're more Hugo's age than mine."

"Hugo's invited, too," her dad said. "And I hear there's an older kid staying with them as well. A nephew or something. I got the impression he's kind of a sullen customer. Bit of a delinquent. He sounds more like your type."

Cass glared. "Thanks for trying to fix me up with some sociopath, Dad. And how are we supposed to get there? It's miles away."

"Take the aluminum boat."

"You know I don't approve of using the outboard. It's

polluting. But..." She considered it. "It is only nine-and-a-half horsepower. And we could get there way faster than sailing."

"And didn't you say they had a collection of native things?" I asked.

"Yeah, that's right." Cass brightened. "We can ask to see them. Maybe it won't be so bad after all. Though I doubt it."

"That's a *cottage*?" I shouted over the noise of the motor. At the top of a vast lawn sat a huge log house with a slate roof and many chimneys.

"Amazing, eh?" Cass shouted back. "Some rich Americans built it a long time ago, when the railway was supposed to go through. This lake was going to be a big resort area. The railway never got built, though, and nobody came. Dad says Mrs. Bonnycastle's father got the house for peanuts."

She eased the boat alongside the dock. I climbed out and gazed around in wonder. Cass tied the boat up and started up the flagstone path, which had shrubs and flower beds on either side. It seemed so strange, this civilized place in the middle of nowhere.

I stopped in my tracks. "Look at that!" The bushes had been trimmed into fancy shapes—globes and birds and animals, like something out of *Alice in Wonderland*.

"Dad says they've been cutting them that way since he was a kid," Cass said.

The path ended at a circular drive. We stopped. A police car was parked outside the front door of the house.

While we were deciding what to do, the door opened. Out came two officers, a man and a woman. They walked down the steps, said good morning to us, got in their car and drove away.

"Maybe somebody's been murdered," said Hugo.

"I guess we might as well find out what's going on," Cass said.

The door-knocker was shaped like a leering gargoyle. Cass grasped it by the nose and clanked it. The door was opened at once by a scowling dark-haired woman. She wasn't at all how I'd pictured Mrs. Bonnycastle.

"Hi, Carmen," said Cass. "Mrs. B. invited us over to see Roger and Anne-Sophie."

Reluctantly, the woman stood aside to let us in.

The squeaking of our rubber soles on the shiny tiles was deafening in the quiet hall. "Is she the *maid*?" I whispered.

"Housekeeper," Cass whispered back.

Carmen ushered us into a room. "Your visitors, Meesus Bonnycastle."

"*Merci*, Carmen." The voice came from the sofa, where a lady with sleek black hair was reading a magazine. Her mouth was bright red and her eyebrows were thin and black. She was wearing an expensive-looking silky outfit. Mom had made us change into clean clothes, but we were still pretty grungy in our shorts and dirty runners.

"I believe you are twice as big as last year, Cass." Mrs. Bonnycastle's voice was lilting and musical, her accent French. "Your friend Amy is not with you this summer?"

"She's in Vancouver," Cass muttered. "These are my new friends, Leia and Hugo."

Mrs. Bonnycastle turned to us. "The children of Rose Greenway! You are lucky to have so talented a mother."

"Thank you," I said. I liked it when people knew who Mom was. "We are."

"We saw a police car outside," said Hugo. "Everybody okay?"

Mrs. B's face changed. "It is very upsetting. We have had a robbery."

"That's terrible," Cass said. "Just now?"

"Three days ago. The children and I had not yet arrived from Ottawa. Only the caretakers and my nephew were here. Carmen and Manuel heard the thieves leaving in a boat."

"A boat? That's a new one. Did they take much?" Cass asked.

"Televisions and computers. Other things that could be easily sold. Some of my husband's artifacts."

Cass looked dismayed. "Oh, no!"

"Only some." Mrs. Bonnycastle waved her hand. "I'm sure I don't know who would want those old things. Though some are very valuable, of course. It is the idea that distresses me. The violation. But enough of this." She stood up. "Come and see the children. They are very excited you are coming."

Her heels clicked across the floor, and gold bangles jingled on her arm. We followed her two doors down the hall. "Roger, Anne-Sophie," she cried. "Your visitors!"

A boy and a girl looked up from a video game. The boy was ten or eleven, with a pale, round face. His sister looked the same, only younger. She had near-white hair in two ponytails high on her head, held in place with pink clips.

"Here is Cass to see you," said Mrs. Bonnycastle. "And some new friends, Leia and Hugo."

The two kids said hello, but their eyes strayed back to their game.

"And this is my nephew, Paul."

A boy with a headset and Discman got up from a couch in the corner. He seemed about Tim's age. His hair was long and dark, bleached at the ends, and he wore a black T-shirt and baggy jeans. He nodded briefly at us. "Pleased to meet you. Sorry, Aunt Helene, I gotta go." He nearly ran out of the room.

Mrs. Bonnycastle threw up her hands. "That boy! Where does he have to go? There is nowhere here to go!" She shook her head. "Well, I will leave you to get on with your playing. Carmen will bring you some refreshments." She floated out the door.

Roger and Anne-Sophie had already returned to their game. Hugo sidled in next to them.

"I see the burglars didn't get your Nintendo," Cass said.

"This one is from home," said Roger. "It's an Xbox, not a Nintendo."

She opened a cupboard. "Your telescope's still here. Can I show Hugo and Leia?"

"It's not dark out."

"I *know* that. We weren't going to look at the *stars*. What are these?" She held up a wooden box.

"Microscope slides. Daddy brought them from the museum."

"We could look at them. It doesn't have to be dark to see microscope slides."

"You spilled last time," said Anne-Sophie. "Water got in the drawers. Mama said—"

"I don't remember spilling anything," Cass snapped.

"Flowers," said Roger, clicking at the screen.

"Oh, yeah. Stupid place for them," Cass muttered. "Okay, can I show my friends your father's collection in the library?"

"Guess so," Roger said doubtfully. "The police went in there already."

Hugo was hunkered firmly in front of the game. I followed Cass down the hall. "Wait till you see this," she said over her shoulder. She stopped in front of an open doorway and waved me in.

It was a fantastic room—long tables, leather chairs, lamps with green glass shades. One whole wall was French doors overlooking the lawn and the lake. The other walls had floor-to-ceiling bookshelves and old photographs and paintings, glass cases of peace pipes and stuffed birds and animals and arrowheads. On a long oak table sat a bronze Indian head, wearing a feathered headdress. My jaw dropped.

Cass looked pleased by my reaction. "Wild, eh? Lots of the things are from western tribes, but some come from around here. That's what I wanted to show you. Mrs. Bonnycastle's father started the collection, and Mr. Bonnycastle added to it. He says it's mostly second-rate, but I think it's fantastic. And see this?" I followed her across the carpet to the shelves. "The books are under headings, like in a real library."

I pointed to empty spots along one wall. "That must be where things were stolen from. Maybe we shouldn't be touching anything. The police might still be checking for fingerprints."

"I don't see any crime-scene tape."

I went up and down the shelves, looking for books on the Algonkins. After a while I found a section marked "Eastern Woodland Peoples," but a high-backed armchair was in the way. I shoved it, but it didn't budge. Someone was sitting in it.

"Oh, sorry!"

The boy that Mrs. Bonnycastle had introduced as her nephew turned down the volume on his Discman. "S'all right."

"Roger and Anne-Sophie said it was okay to come in," Cass said.

"It's their house. Go right ahead." He didn't sound like he meant it, though. I went back to looking at the books. When I stole a glimpse at him, he was tapping his foot, lost in the music.

But a few minutes later he sat up. "You hear that?"

"Hear what?" It was hard to imagine that he could hear anything over the music. But he was already on his way out the French doors.

Three seconds later Mrs. Bonnycastle bustled in, her arms full of flowers. "Oh! I did not expect to find anyone here."

"Hugo's with Roger and Anne-Sophie," Cass said quickly. "They said it was okay to show Leia Mr. Bonnycastle's collection and books. We weren't disturbing anything, in case the police are coming back."

"No, they are finished." Mrs. Bonnycastle began arranging her flowers in a vase. "Certainly, look at the books. There are so many. My husband cannot bear to be away from books, even when he is on vacation."

"Is he here?" Cass asked.

"No, he is too busy working, working."

"Sorry to hear that. Well, say hello to him for me. We should probably go see how the others are getting on."

But Mrs. Bonnycastle wasn't finished sharing her thoughts. "I do not come here to work. I come for the peace and beauty of nature. Of course, it is different if you are young. You like to have excitement and things to do. Waterskiing and Jet Skis."

"We don't," Cass protested. "I hate those things."

"My children are not interested in such things either. They are happy with their computers and games. But to have friends is also important, I tell them. So you must come and visit whenever you wish."

We edged to the door and escaped. Down the hall Hugo was eating chips, still watching Roger and Anne-Sophie play their game. He wouldn't budge until it was finished. We had to drag him back to the boat. "We were hardly there any time at all," he complained.

72

"Too bad Mrs. Bonnycastle had to butt in before you got a good look at the library," Cass said to me. "And that Paul, too. He's horrible."

"I didn't think he was so bad. He just doesn't like being around his aunt."

"Whatever. He wasn't exactly friendly, was he? I'm surprised he was in the library. He seems more a Stephen King kind of guy."

"He wasn't reading Stephen King." He'd left his book in the chair. "He was reading about Indian burials and ghost spirits."

"Leia saw an Indian ghost," Hugo told Cass.

She stopped walking and looked at me. "What ghost?"

I made a silent vow to never share a secret with Hugo again. "I don't really know if it was a ghost," I said, embarrassed. "It was just a *ghostly* experience. One minute it was there, and the next it disappeared."

"You're not allowed to tell Tim," Hugo told Cass.

"Why not?"

"He'd say I was out in the sun too long," I explained. Tim didn't believe in ghosts. He didn't even believe in horoscopes.

Cass nodded. "Well, Tim would say that. But what do *you* think you saw? I'd love to see a ghost, but I never have," she added enviously. "Maybe you're psychic."

For a moment I thought of telling her about my vision through the cottage door, but then I changed my mind. It was just too complicated.

Nine

❧

THE NEXT MORNING, TIM, HUGO AND I met Cass down at her dock. She and her dad had put the sails on their boat, and it bobbed on the waves, gleaming and golden. "See?" she said. "Just the same as yours."

"Ours doesn't look like that," said Hugo.

"It will, if Tim ever gets it done. Hop in."

"Hugo and I haven't sailed before," I reminded her. "Only Tim has." I felt kind of nervous. Sailboats could tip.

"Just do what Tim says, then. He's the captain."

We all managed to squeeze in, and Tim handed Hugo and me each a rope. I clutched mine, anxious to do the right thing. "Hugo, you're in charge of the foresail, and Leia's in charge of the main," Tim said. "I'll tell you when to pull on them."

Cass pushed us off and I waited for something to happen.

Nothing much did. The sails flapped and we moved slowly out of the bay. It was a nice sunny day and the water smelled wonderful, but this was sailing? It wasn't exactly as exciting as I had expected.

Tim pointed at a patch of ripples coming toward us. "That's what we want. Let your rope out more, Leia." The sails filled a little and the boat began to speed up.

"What about my rope?" Hugo asked.

"When I tell you." We surged ahead, the water making a rushing noise against the bottom of the boat.

"It's a good wind, now that we're out of the lee of the shore," Cass said. "You should be able to get across the bay in a couple of tacks."

74

"Is this a test?" Tim asked suspiciously.

She looked indignant. "Of course not."

"We'll be coming about in a minute," Tim told us. "That means we'll change direction. When I shout, keep your heads down, or you'll get hit by the boom."

"What's a boom?" Hugo asked.

"The big piece of wood along the bottom of the mainsail," Tim said. "It's called a boom because of the noise it makes when it hits you. Okay, coming about!" He shoved the tiller hard over to one side. "Duck!"

There was a lot of confusion as we all dove for the bottom at once.

"Ow!" Hugo didn't get his head down fast enough.

"That didn't sound like a boom," Cass said. "More a clunk, actually."

Hugo scowled, rubbing his head, but he didn't seem to be bleeding. I was, though. Somehow, I'd managed to skin my knee.

"Not bad for a first tack, but your crew could use a little practice," Cass told Tim.

When we rounded the point, I got my first view of our destination. Cass pointed. "Head for that cliff."

It was impressive, like the side had fallen off the hill, leaving a rock wall forty feet high. Cass directed Tim toward a pebbly beach to one side. Then she jumped out and dragged us into shore. "Not a bad landing," she said to Tim. If it *was* a test, I guess he did okay.

Cass had a spot picked out where we could hunt for arrowheads. Her father knew the farmer, she said, and he wouldn't mind us searching on his land. She led the way across the rocks toward the cliff. "The fields are just over the top."

"We're not going up there, are we?" Hugo asked. He wasn't crazy about heights.

"It's not that high. Me and Amy used to come over here to climb all the time. It's fun." Once we reached the bottom of the cliff, Cass was up it like a mountain goat. She looked back at us and grinned. "Look up now, but don't look down later."

I tightened the straps of my backpack and started up. It was easy enough at first, until the rock ledge got narrower and there weren't any bushes to grab. Cass was already at the top. She leaned over to coach me.

"There's a trick to it, Leia. Move your left foot onto that bit that juts out. Then reach your right hand up to the ledge above you. Then just pull yourself up. It's not that dangerous."

It felt dangerous, though, with nothing but jagged rocks between me and the water below. My fingers were slippery with sweat. Only a few more seconds, I told myself. Only a few more steps and the ordeal would be over—one way or another. I gritted my teeth and took one step, then another. Cass reached down and grabbed my wrist. I was at the top.

She hugged me. "You did it!"

"Not very well." But I felt proud of myself all the same.

Tim had let Hugo go ahead of him, and by now they were past the halfway point. But Hugo wasn't going anywhere—up or down. He had come to a complete stop, paralyzed with fear. His face was pinched and white. Below him were the rocks.

We coaxed and pleaded, but it had no effect. Cass looked at her watch. "He hasn't budged for fifteen minutes. Maybe I should go around the long way and get some rope from the boat," she said. "If he falls—"

Hugo heard her and groaned.

"If you do fall, I'll push you out so you land in the water," Tim said.

"Tim!" I looked down at poor Hugo. If possible, he was even whiter than before. "Get the rope," he croaked up at me and Cass.

"You don't need a rope," Cass said. "You can do it. Move your feet along a bit."

Hugo stayed rooted to the spot. "Get a helicopter."

"Try, at least, Hugo," I begged. "Move your foot a tiny bit."

At last he took a deep breath. Slowly, slowly, he inched his foot along.

"Well done! Now the other one," said Cass.

Another deep breath and he shuffled farther along, one foot, then the other, until his toe bumped the outcrop. He yelped, his eyes round with terror.

"You're doing fantastic." Cass grabbed him by the wrist. He clambered frantically upward. His heel slipped, sending loose rock skittering down the cliff.

His foot was still waving in space, but Cass had him and she dragged him over the top. He stood up, walked quickly away from the edge and threw up.

"You okay?" I called down to Tim.

"Yeah, except for the face full of stones."

Tim reached the top without needing a hand. Hugo was sitting in the grass, drinking water from his bottle. His face was still pale. Tim went over and squatted in front of him. "Sorry, buddy. We won't ever make you do that again."

"Yeah, sorry about that," said Cass. "It's got nothing to do with being brave. You're either afraid of heights or you're not. Here, have some of these."

Hugo stared at the squished red things in her hand.

"Wild strawberries," she said. "There's tons." The hillside was covered in berries, no bigger than a taste, tiny and sweet. We picked them straight into our mouths, staining our fingers red.

When we'd eaten our fill, we drank some water and set off across the hilltop toward the fields. I looked longingly back at the lake. It was so hot that my shirt stuck to my back. Spiny blue flowers and yellow ones on long stalks swam in the heat. The thistles scratched white tracks on my legs. It felt like being in the desert.

Cass startled me, grabbing my arm. "Yikes!"

"What is it?"

"Snake," she said weakly. I glimpsed a slender tail whipping through the grass.

Hugo ran ahead. "A garter snake. Want me to catch it?"

"No!"

He wouldn't have been able to anyway. It disappeared into the ground.

"Don't worry, there are no poisonous snakes in this part of the country," Tim told Cass. "They're extinct."

"I don't care if they're extinct or not. They give me the creeps."

I eased her fingers off my arm. She'd been clutching so hard they'd left marks.

"Don't worry, Cass," said Hugo. "It got away...this time." He scraped his foot on the grass. "Yuck. I stepped in a cow pie."

Tim stopped. "There are cows?"

"Usually," said Cass. "But just cows, no bulls."

Tim began walking faster. He was the first to reach the fence.

"He doesn't like cows," Hugo confided. "He's afraid they'll chase him."

Cass grinned. "Yo, Tim!" she called after him. "Cows aren't poisonous."

"But they're dangerous, as far as he's concerned," I said. "When we used to go to Gran's house in the country, there was a cow next door that hated Tim. It ran after him once and tossed him in a ditch."

From the crest of the hill we could see the field. It had been plowed and then left—half bare earth and half weeds. "Dad used to find arrowheads here when he was a kid," Cass said.

"How would arrowheads get here?" Tim asked.

"Hunters shooting at deer and stuff, I guess. Iroquois on the warpath."

"Hope we don't find any skulls," said Hugo.

"Where should we start digging?" I asked.

"We don't have to dig," said Cass. "That's the whole point. We just see what the plow's turned up."

We fanned out across the field, our eyes on the ground. Hugo kept pace with me, kicking the edges off furrows. I picked up things that turned out to be only sticks or stones. We got all the way to the other side of the field without finding anything except a scrap that might have been pottery—unless it was soft rock. I put it in my pack.

Across the field Tim was calling out and waving. "He's found something, Hugo," I said. "We'd better search harder."

Hugo pointed. "What about over there?" On the other side of the fence was a field planted with corn.

We wriggled through the wire. The sun was still boiling hot, but the sea of green corn stalks around us made it seem a little cooler. And from the next rise we could see the lake again. Way in the distance I could pick out our cottages—squares of dark green half-hidden in the trees. Beyond that and to the right, over near Half Moon Bay, a cloud of brown dust rose in the air. I could hear rumbling like distant thunder.

Hugo spotted some yellow earthmoving machine making the dust. "It's a Caterpillar," he said. "It's building a road." We watched for a while and then walked on. Suddenly Hugo dropped to his knees. "Hey, I found something! An arrowhead!" He rubbed the dirt off on his shorts.

Finally! "Let me see." I took it and turned it in my hand, scratching away more of the dirt with my fingernail. It was an arrowhead, all right—our very first one. The edges were delicately cut, the point still sharp enough to hurt when I pressed it against my skin. "It's really good. It's even got notches where it tied onto the arrow."

Hugo put it carefully in his pack.

As I reached for my water bottle, I became aware of another noise, a lot closer than the earthmoving machine. It was an engine. And a dog was barking. "Hugo, look!" On the far side of the field a tractor had driven up to the gate. A man on the tractor was waving his fist at us. A German shepherd bounded toward us through the rows. This didn't look good. "Run!"

We tore back through the field the way we'd come. That man wouldn't drive his tractor after us, would he? He'd knock down all his corn. But the dog was still coming, barking its head off. We scurried through the rows of waist-high corn as fast as we could go.

"Keep your head down, Hugo!" Staying out of sight would help with the man on the tractor. Of course, the dog was another story.

At the top of the hill, Hugo stood up. "It's stopped barking. I can't see it."

"Stay down!" I could hear panting now—and it wasn't mine.

Suddenly the dog appeared at one end of the row—big and black, galloping toward us, tongue lolling. It began barking again. This time running wouldn't help. We froze.

The dog stopped a few feet away from us, barking

furiously. Saliva dripped from its jaws. I shrank away in terror.

But Hugo stuck out his hand. "Hey, boy," he said in a coaxing voice. "Come here, boy."

"Hugo, no, he'll bite you!"

"No, he won't. He's friendly. See? His tail's wagging. Good boy." The dog didn't seem particularly friendly to me, but Hugo reached out his hand for him to sniff. He barked a few more times, then stopped.

"What's your name, boy?" The dog didn't answer, but he did sit, cocking his head quizzically to one side.

Hugo dug in his pack. "I'm gonna give him some of my sandwich. You hungry, boy?" He unwrapped his lunch and took a bite. The dog eyed him with interest and Hugo passed him the rest. That sandwich disappeared in one gulp.

Now that Hugo and the dog were buddies, our only problem was getting rid of him. As we made our way back to the fence, Hugo showed him the empty wrapper. "That's all, boy." But still the dog followed right along behind us, wagging his tail. When we told him to go home, he hung his head, looking hurt. I think the only reason he finally did leave was that he heard his owner whistling for him.

Cass and Tim were waiting for us in the first field. "What happened to you?"

"We got shouted at by a man on a tractor," said Hugo. "We weren't hurting the crummy corn. He had a nice dog, though."

"Must have been Duffault, or one of his sons," said Cass. "I'll ask Dad to explain next time he goes over to buy vegetables. But did you find anything?"

Hugo took out his arrowhead. Cass and Tim were impressed. "It hardly even looks used," Tim said.

I'd brought my camera, and I took a picture of the arrowhead in Hugo's hand to show the scale. Cass had found an arrowhead, too, with the point broken off, and Tim had collected a bunch of little pieces of pottery. I photographed them as well. Unfortunately, everybody decided that the rock I'd picked up was just a rock.

There was no way Hugo was going to go back down that cliff, so Cass showed us a different route back to the boat, through another field. Tim found a peculiar stone, about eight inches long and rounded on one end. Cass thought it might have been used for grinding corn. But Hugo's perfect arrowhead found on enemy soil was still the prize of the day.

Ten

WITH CASS AROUND ALL THE TIME NOW, there was lots more going on. I hardly got a chance to read anymore. We swam and canoed, and after we found those artifacts in the field, we got serious about searching for more. There was only one problem: We didn't want to go back to the Duffaults' fields and get yelled at again. I wanted to go back to the old Indian village in Half Moon Bay, but that would mean going past the horrible skull stump again.

Cass thought we should at least take another look. "It was just a bunch of old litter," she argued, sitting on our porch while we finished breakfast.

"It was sinister," I said.

"I'm not going back," said Hugo. "That scary junk monster winked at me."

"And we know that's not possible, right?" said Cass reasonably. "We need to go back for a second look. There's enough breeze to sail across now."

I was up for it, but—as usual—Tim wasn't. Mom was driving to Pembroke to do some shopping, and he wanted to go and buy supplies to finish the boat. Hugo thought he might like to go, too. "I want to do some skateboarding," he said, "and I want to get another Nintendo game."

"You've spent all your money, and your birthday isn't for another few weeks," said Mom. "You stay with the girls."

I wasn't as nervous about sailing this time. The sails filled up right away, and the water made that rushing noise against the bottom of the boat before we were even out of our bay.

Cass stretched out, the tiller across her lap. "Want some of this?" She reached out a finger to smear blue sunblock on my nose, and then lay back and let out a contented sigh. "Isn't this fantastic? Poor old Amy stuck in Vancouver. I got a postcard saying it's been raining since she got there." She held up one leg. "I'm determined to get a tan this summer. Do you think I should shave my legs?"

"You don't really need to," I said enviously. Her leg hair was fine and coppery. Ever since I started shaving my legs a year ago, I had to do it all the time or I got stubble thick as pencil leads.

"I might shave mine," said Hugo. "Some guys do, you know. Less wind resistance on my skateboard."

"Is Amy a good sailor?" I asked Cass.

"Amy's a *great* sailor, way better than me. We'd be going twice as fast as this, and Amy'd be hanging out so far, her butt would be in the water." She laughed.

And I was just sitting there like a lump with a rope in my hand, wondering whether I should pull on it.

"Coming about!" Cass yelled. After a lot of knee scraping across the bottom of the boat, we were finally approaching shore. In fact, I was afraid we were going to sail right into it. At the last minute Cass pushed the tiller hard over, and the boat glided into a calm stretch.

"Okay, let out the sails." She pulled up the centerboard. "Hugo, you paddle us in."

He grabbed the paddle, but it wasn't as easy as he figured. The boat kept going one way, then the other. The tip of his paddle caught a wave, flinging water into the air. Most of it landed on Cass.

He turned around when he heard her shriek. Water trickled off her chin, and her hair and T-shirt were soaked.

"Uh-oh," he said, looking more than a little worried. But Cass didn't seem to mind being half-drowned. She sent him over the side to tie the bowline to a tree and then threw an anchor off the stern.

Again we walked through the birches and cedars and on into the pines. The closer we got to the clearing, the slower Hugo went.

"Stop dragging your feet and don't be a baby," Cass said. "It's just a heap of junk."

"But it winked at me!"

When we got to the top of the cliff, we walked around the strange construction, giving it a wide berth. The skull was still on the top. Cass pointed. "Aha!"

The mirrored sunglasses had fallen off and we could see a robin's nest inside the skull. The mother robin flapped away, and I saw a bunch of baby robin heads sticking up, all of them squawking. "There's your winking eye, Hugo," Cass said. "A bird!"

So it was just a junk collage after all. But the thing was still creepy. Who made it? And why?

Cass was already heading toward the log cabin. From the outside, at least, it seemed deserted. She peered through a dusty window. "I can see a table."

Hugo rattled the doorknob. "Hey, it's not locked." He pushed it open.

"People should be more careful," said Cass. "They could get broken into, like the Bonnycastles."

"I don't think we should go in," I said, but it was too late. Hugo and Cass were already inside.

There wasn't much furniture—only two chairs, a table and a daybed. Some yellowing pictures were tacked to the log walls, and a woodstove sat in one corner. "It's really neat," Cass said. "Tidy, I mean."

Tidy, like somebody lived there. Hugo opened a

cupboard. "Food!" Cans of soup and stew and condensed milk were stacked two rows high. He picked up a plastic bag. "A loaf of bread."

I took it and squeezed it. It wasn't even stale. "Somebody's living here, you guys. I told you we shouldn't come in."

"Omigod, it's like in *Goldilocks and the Three Bears*," cried Cass. "Let's get out before we break the bed!"

Hugo was first across the room. He got to the doorway and then stopped in his tracks. "Uh-oh, somebody's coming."

"Quit blocking the door!" I tried to see past him and caught a glimpse of a shaggy figure walking slowly up the path. He had a stick in one hand and a rifle in the other.

"He's got a gun!"

There were no other exits, no closets, no more rooms. We piled out, almost flattening an old man in the stampede. He looked very angry.

Partway down the rocky hillside Hugo tripped on a root and went sprawling. He started making an awful noise. "Shut up, Hugo!" I hissed. "You're not bleeding."

"I bruised myself!"

I looked over my shoulder, but the old man wasn't following us. "He didn't shoot. He yelled and shook his stick, but he's not chasing us."

"How come we have to keep running away all the time?"

"Because we keep being in the wrong place at the wrong time." I was still panting for breath.

"Where's Cass?" he asked.

"She was right behind me." She was the last out the door. "Cass?" I called. "Cass!" We stared up toward the cabin, listening. No answer. I felt sick. "We have to go back, Hugo. Cass could get killed!"

86

"I didn't hear any shots."

"Well, we can't just stand here."

"Maybe we should call the police," Hugo called after me fearfully.

"You bring a cell phone?" I didn't mention that without Cass we wouldn't even be able to get home. We couldn't sail. We were marooned.

The baby birds in the cow skull watched us scuttle past. We stopped outside the cabin. The door was shut now. Everything was quiet—too quiet. I couldn't hear anything except my own ragged breathing.

"What if he killed her?" Hugo whispered hoarsely. "I wish Tim was here."

We crept toward the door. Suddenly it opened, and I jumped back with a little shriek.

The old man's face was in the shadows, so I couldn't make out his expression. He motioned for us to come in. I shook my head and reached for Hugo's hand.

Cass appeared behind him. "It's okay." She didn't seem to be hurt. "I stayed behind to apologize."

"You all come in and sit down, eh?" the old man said. "Only two chairs, but plenty bed an' floor."

Cass grinned and nodded at us. I stepped nervously through the door. Hugo shuffled in behind me.

The old man lowered himself into the chair beside the stove. His rifle leaned against the wall behind him. Over his plaid shirt he wore a fringed leather vest. He had shaggy white hair and a white beard. The light from the window fell on a lined face and eyes that gazed out under bristling eyebrows. It was those strange, almost black eyes that made him look so fierce.

I squirmed under the stare. "We're awfully sorry about breaking into your house."

"We didn't know anybody lived here," Hugo added.

The old man waved his hand. "No bother. Don't worry about it no more. This young lady stay an' explain to me. Maybe I put up a sign: 'Marcel, 'e live 'ere. Back soon.' Now, sit down an' stay for a while." Hugo and I sat on the bed.

"I was just asking Marcel how long he's lived here," said Cass.

"Long time," he said. "Very long time. I been telling her I first come 'ere maybe seventy years, when I was born."

"Are you a hermit?" Hugo asked.

"No, no. I don't live all that time in this place. I live different places, some time here, some time other place. Now I jus' want to stay on my own land. Grow my garden, sit in de sun."

"What about in the winter?" Cass asked. "Do you live here, too?"

"Winter not so good. If cold don't get me, cabin fever does." His eyes moved from one of us to the next, sizing us up. "You boy an' girls from de city? What you come looking around for?"

"Indians," said Hugo.

"We were hoping to find native artifacts," said Cass. "People around here say there used to be a native village on the point, so we were searching for things like arrowheads or pottery."

"Are there live native people still living around here?" I asked. Then I got embarrassed. "Of course they'd be alive if they were living."

He smiled. "I'm alive, I guess. Way back, my great-gran'fadder was Indian chief."

"You're a full-blooded Indian?" Hugo's eyes widened.

"Ha! Not so full-blooded. French, Irish, Scotch—all mix up. One great-great-gran'fadder was fur trader."

88

Across the room the kettle began to rattle and hiss. The old man heaved himself out of his chair. "Tea, boy an' girls?" He filled a tin pot with boiling water.

"Do you have an Indian name?" Hugo asked.

"Marcel Campbell. That sound Indian to you?"

Hugo shook his head.

"Are there any other native people besides you around here?" I asked.

"Only a few. Once many Algonkin 'ere, long time ago, my gran'fadder tell me. More and more come to trade furs. Den, a big sickness—white man's sickness. That camp in de clearing was very big one. White man's sickness wipe nearly everybody out."

"So that's what happened," said Cass.

"An' after that, Iroquois warriors come an' track down most everyone left an' kill dem."

I was horrified. "What for?"

"For our hunting grounds an' fur trade. Our people hide in de woods and starve. Some go wit' de priests. Anyway, everyone forget all that now. They forget this land was always Algonkin hunting ground."

He went to his cupboard. "But this is not happy talk for new friends. I forget my manners." He took down some mugs and glasses and filled them with tea from the pot, thick with leaves. Then he opened a tin of condensed milk and stirred it in. Hugo got his in an old jam jar. "Somebody have to make do with de second-bes' china."

"Is it caffeinated?" Cass asked.

"For sure."

She sipped it warily. "Tastes great." She sounded surprised. "I don't usually like tea."

"Cookie, too? Stale, maybe, but good for dipping." He passed around a bag of gingersnaps and sat down again. "I t'ink you only girls an' boy on dis part of de lake."

"Nearly," said Cass. "There's Leia and Hugo's brother, Tim. He didn't come with us because he's always too busy. And there are two kids around Hugo's age, the Bonnycastles, in that place that used to be a lodge over near the village. But they don't go outside much."

"Like indoor cats," explained Hugo.

"Those two I forgot. But like you say, nobody sees dem. An' that other boy, I think, he come back."

"You know about him?" Cass sounded surprised. "Paul?"

He nodded. "You know him, too? Maybe be friend for you. Must be lonely sometime."

Cass didn't seem impressed at the thought of being friends with Paul. "It's not lonely at all. In fact, this place is getting way overpopulated. There are more cottagers than there used to be. Strangers. Somebody broke into the Bonnycastles' place. You should maybe think about locking your cabin."

"Why I do that? Nothing to take," said Marcel.

Hugo fidgeted beside me. He raised his hand, like in school. "Um, do you hunt for food?"

"Once I did, but no more. Too old to kill now."

"Why do you have a gun then?"

"For 'mergency. I just get that one fixed. Maybe a bear break in for food." He started to get out of his chair again but had to rock back and forth to tip himself onto his feet. "Old bones," he said, reaching for his stick. "Come. I goin' show you somet'ing."

We followed him out and along the path where we'd first seen him, away from the ridge. A little ways on he stopped by a pile of rocks with a piece of plywood on top. He pulled the wood aside, and we peered in. I saw water about three feet down.

Marcel reached for a pail tied to a tree. "Clear-running

spring. Even when it does not rain, she never go dry. I figure this spring is reason Algonkin make rendezvous 'ere."

"You can't live on water," said Hugo. "What do you eat?"

"I fish some. An' Pelletier, he send out supply to me. An' I grow some things." He put the plywood back over the well and led the way farther into the woods to another clearing. In the middle was something like a kid's fort, made of tall spindly poles with chicken wire at the top.

"To keep out deer and rabbits," Marcel explained, unhooking a gate. Behind it was a neat garden plot. Bright green lettuce, ferny carrot tops and radishes sprouted from the black earth.

"How come you don't have weeds?" I asked.

He grinned. "I pull dem out." He showed us which plants were beans, tomatoes and squash. He was even growing corn.

"Everything's much bigger than in our garden," I said.

"Because I water dem lots." He pointed to a row of plastic barrels along one side of the stockade. It was his system for siphoning water onto the garden in dry times. "Not much need dis year so far. But some year, it make all de difference. De soil ver' good. I t'ink maybe Indian people grow t'ings in dis place long time ago."

"I thought Algonkins were hunters," said Cass.

"Dis was big camp, in one place for long time. I t'ink for sure they must grow t'ings."

He led us back out the gate and hooked it shut. When we got back near his cabin I pointed down the ridge to the stump with its strange collection of junk. "Uh, what's that?"

Marcel grinned. "My totem."

"Doesn't look like any totem pole to me," said Hugo.

"*Nindoodem*, the people call it, what we worship. But maybe it looks like garbage to you?"

"Yeah," said Hugo. "Where'd all those things come from?"

"I find dem—floating in de lake, thrown in de woods, beside de road." He went over to it and poked his stick at a ketchup bottle. "Some t'ings, I am responsible for myself. Dey all remind me why I come 'ere. Why I don't live in de city no more."

"We take all that stuff to the dump," said Cass.

"Most t'ings you put in de dump, they don't go away. Jus' you don't see dem no more."

"But they're *ugly*."

He shrugged. "You hunting for t'ings the Indian lef' behind. These t'ings de white man leave behind."

"Yeah, right. I prefer Indian things."

When he waved us off and started back up the track, I called after him, "Thanks for the tea."

"It was excellent," Hugo added.

"*Plaisir*."

We watched him disappear into his cabin. "Okay, he's a little strange, but isn't he great?" Cass crowed as we started back to the canoe. "If it wasn't for me staying behind to apologize, we wouldn't have met him."

"You were brave," I said. "I completely panicked."

"He could've shot you with his gun," said Hugo.

"He was pretty mad at us, for sure. But I explained. I mean, we didn't touch anything that belonged to him."

"We touched his bread," said Hugo.

"He must be the one who owns land around here," she went on thoughtfully. "The name I saw at the registry office. Campbell."

That didn't make sense to me. "You need a lot of money to own land."

"He said his grandfather owned it. He probably inherited it."

"Don't you still have to pay taxes?" I asked.

"Maybe he used to be a hunting guide and made lots of money from rich Americans. He said he lived in the city—maybe he had a job there, too."

"I don't think he's got much money."

"So maybe he has a relative who owns it and lets him stay here. Whatever."

We took one quick turn around the clearing looking for relics. Just as we were heading off toward the boat, Hugo gave a shout. We ran back to see what he'd found. "A spearhead!"

Cass took it.

"Be careful!"

She crumbled it in her hand. "It's just mud."

"My spearhead!" Hugo roared. "You wrecked it!"

"Calm down." Cass patted his head. "They didn't make spearheads out of mud."

The woods were too full of mosquitoes for a picnic, so we paddled the boat out from shore to find a breeze. Cass threw out the anchor and unwrapped a muesli bar. She gave a huge yawn. "I could just stretch out and go to sleep. It's amazing to think I was in Montreal a couple of days ago."

We fed our crumbs to the sunfish and raised sail. This time we were heading into the wind. It was sort of exciting to see how far we could get before Cass shouted, "Coming about!"

Halfway across the bay, a torpedo-shaped speedboat roared past, towing a water-skier. The white-haired man in a captain's hat at the wheel waved to us. So did two pretty girls in bikinis.

"Cool," said Hugo.

"Jerks," Cass muttered. She turned the bow into the wake. "Hang on tight." The *Arrow* headed up one side of a wave and came down the other with a bang. It knocked the wind out of our sails. "Haul 'em in," she ordered.

The speedboat was circling again, but everybody in it—including the driver—was watching the skier. They weren't paying any attention to where they were going—and the boat was heading straight for us. "Cass, what should we do?" I cried.

"Nothing," she said calmly. "We have the right-of-way. Sail over power. They have to get out of the road, not us. It's lake rules."

But the big boat didn't seem to know lake rules. Seconds away from a collision, Cass shoved the tiller hard over. The *Arrow* turned—the boom swinging, the sails flapping in our faces. At the same moment the speedboat's driver saw us and swerved. He missed us by yards.

The girl skiing behind was still zooming toward us, though. With a scream she let go of the rope. I didn't see what happened next, because the *Arrow* bounced in the air, knocking me into the bottom on top of Hugo. When I got back up, I saw the girl treading water. We'd missed her.

The boat swung back in a wide arc to pick up the fallen skier. The man at the wheel was so close I could see the curly gray hair on his tanned chest.

Cass stood up. "Sail over power, you aging nymphomaniac!" she shrieked.

"Sit down, Cass!"

"He should be arrested," she yelled, shaking her fist at the boat. "Lake rules, you moron!"

I grabbed the seat of her shorts. "No standing up in a boat, Cass! You said! Lake rules!"

"Okay, okay." She sat down. Her face was white. "It's

a miracle there isn't blood and guts all over the bay. We could have run right into that girl. They could have rammed us. Dumb city jerks!"

Tim met us at Cass's dock and helped us tie up. "Did you see that moron cut us off?" Cass asked him, still pale and shaking with anger. "People without brains shouldn't be allowed on this lake."

"I saw them get the girl out of the water," Tim said. "She was okay. Everybody survived—even the moron."

"Well, maybe he shouldn't have," said Cass darkly.

"Where's the Indian stuff you were going to find?" Tim asked, switching to a safer topic.

"Didn't find any," Hugo said. "We found a live Indian, though."

I told Tim about Marcel. "He has native ancestry, but he's Quebecois as well."

"He's living in the woods?" Tim frowned. "How come you went into his house?"

"He's not a pervert, if that's what you're thinking," said Cass. "The first time we went in was a mistake. The second time, he invited us. He's a really nice old guy."

"That's what he wants you to think, anyway," said Tim.

Cass turned on him. "Listen, you've got no right to offer an opinion like that! You weren't there. We were."

"Okay, okay," Tim said, backing down. "Don't get your knickers in a knot. Why don't you go and have a nice cool drink."

"Yeah, Cass, come on." I could see she was still upset from the near accident. It was not a good moment for Tim to pick a fight with her. "You deserve a drink. You saved our lives."

Eleven

"WHAT'S A NYMPHOMANIAC?" Hugo asked at supper-time.

Mom's eyes widened. "A what, Hugo?"

"That's what Cass called the man driving the water-ski boat, Mom," I explained hastily.

"Cass was clearly a little word-challenged in her excitement," Mom said. "But I think we can assume she didn't approve of his taking those girls waterskiing."

Cass phoned after supper when Tim and I were doing dishes. She was whispering, so at first I could hardly hear her. "Are you guys up for a secret mission tonight?" I guess she didn't want her dad to hear.

"Maybe," I said cautiously. "What is it?"

"We're going to knock down that sign."

"What sign?"

"Pelletier's. We should have done it the first day I got back. Pelletier just encourages people like that moron who nearly killed us today. He even rents out Jet Skis! Are you in?"

"Um—I guess so."

"Tell Tim he has to come. We need his muscle."

But Tim didn't want anything to do with Cass's mission. And no amount of begging on my part was going to change his mind. "You don't have to do everything she says."

"Come on, Tim, you have to. Cass will be really disappointed."

"So?" Tim kept on wiping plates. "Anyway, what's the

point? The Pelletiers will think it's just kids who haven't got anything better to do. And they'll be right."

"I'll come," said Hugo. "I'm strong."

"Yeah, all sixty pounds of you," Tim scoffed.

"I weigh more than that." He flexed the biceps on one skinny arm.

"Please, Tim?"

"Drop it, Leia. I don't feel like being bossed around tonight."

"Cass isn't bossing you. She's just being a leader," I said, sticking up for her. "Anyway, she saved our lives today. We owe it to her."

"She didn't save your life—she nearly killed you. I was watching. What was the matter with her anyway? Was she asleep or what? She had plenty of time to get you out of the way."

"We weren't the ones who were supposed to get out of the way—the other guys were. Sail goes before steam—it's lake rules."

"And that's worth dying for?" Tim hung up his dish-towel and walked out of the kitchen.

So just Hugo, Cass and I went on the secret mission. I told Mom we were going for a walk, and we ran up and met Cass in her driveway. "What's Tim's problem any-way?" she asked as we set off.

"He still gets really tired after his chicken pox," I lied.

She bought it. "How long will it take before he's back to normal again?"

"I don't know. I'm sure he'll be fine by August. That's when we go to stay with Dad. Tim's supposed to be help-ing him build a new bathroom."

"I'm all better," said Hugo. "Except my legs are getting tired. How far is it now?"

"Just around the corner," Cass told him.

"We're going to smash the sign, right?" asked Hugo.

"To smithereens. Or at least knock it down."

"Remember, you're sworn to secrecy," I reminded Hugo. "Mom doesn't need to know."

"My dad either," said Cass. "Though I don't think he'd really mind. He's always saying Pelletier overcharges summer people. It's not like we're tourists. My family's been here for three generations. We pay taxes just like Pelletier does."

Three corners later, we came out at the dirt road to the village. There was the sign, nailed to the old rail fence on the other side. It was big, with a round Pepsi sign at the top—black letters on a fluorescent orange background.

LEON PELLETIER
RUE MAIN STREET, LAC WASAMAK LAKE
EPICERIE BOUCHERIE BOULANGERIE
GROCERY BUTCHER BAKERY
SKI-DOO, BOAT AND CABIN RENTALS/A LOUER
613-330-9999

"It's bad enough they put it up at all," said Cass. "But right at the end of our drive—that's asking for it. Okay, attack!"

We were in mid-charge across the road when Cass skidded to a halt, holding up her hand in warning. "Car coming!" We retreated a little way back up the drive to wait for the car to pass.

It didn't, though. It braked and slowed, then rattled to a halt. Doors opened and then slammed shut. "What are they stopping for?" Cass muttered.

I heard men's voices. Had they seen us? We hadn't done anything wrong. Not yet, anyway. More loud talking. The clank of a beer can bouncing off a rock and the smell of cigarettes. A mosquito buzzed in my ear. Then I heard hammering.

Cass edged cautiously up the lane to see what was happening. "This is incredible," she hissed. "They're putting up *another* sign!" She strode forward. Hugo and I followed. A dust-coated truck with rusty fenders was pulled up on the side of the road, and two men were nailing another sign to the fence, right next to the first one. A big guy and a skinny one. Both wearing ball caps over mullet haircuts. I couldn't see their faces, but there was something familiar about them. Maybe it was the roll of bare flesh hanging over the big one's jeans.

Our carpenters. Matt and Lenny.

Cass stood with her hands on her hips, gazing at the new sign. It was even bigger than the other one:

COMING SOON!
WATERFRONT TRAILER COMMUNITY EXCLUSIVE
SITES FULLY SERVICED
CONVENIENCE STORE   PIZZA   WATERSLIDE
BAIE HALF-MOON
613-330-4295

"What's all this about?" Cass demanded loudly. "Half Moon Bay? What trailer community?"

The big one—Matt—pushed back his cap and grinned at her. "Don't ask us, honey. It ain't ours, anyway. We're just hanging a sign." That hairy stomach bulged between his dirt-stained sweatshirt and ancient jeans.

"Well, whose is it, then?"

He headed toward the truck. "Who's askin'?"

"I am."

Lenny was staring at Cass's chest. Then he turned and gave me the up and down, too.

"You ladies lookin' to party?" Matt asked. "How about a beer?"

"They don't look legal to me," growled Lenny.

"So how old are you little gals, anyhow? Sweet sixteen going on twenty-one, eh?"

"I'm fourteen and she's thirteen, if it's any of your business," said Cass. "Hugo's eight. And you didn't answer my question: Who's building the trailer park?"

Matt pointed at the sign. "There's the phone number, sweetheart. Why don't you give them a call and find out? You can have my number, too, if you want." He leered at her and tossed his hammer into the back of the truck. Then he opened the door on the driver's side. When Lenny jumped in, too, Matt honked the horn and blew a kiss as he drove off. Another beer can arced into the air and landed in the middle of the road.

"Jerks," Cass muttered. "Just following orders. Yeah, like the Nazis."

We stared glumly at the two signs, the old one and the alarming new one beside it. "We can't even knock them down, because those lowlifes saw us," she fumed. "What unbelievable timing. The whole thing is completely weird."

"Know what's even weirder?" I said. "That was Matt and Lenny!"

"You mean—"

"The evil unhandymen."

"You're kidding."

Hugo was reading out the new sign to himself. His face lit up. "Hey, pizza. And a waterslide—that would be cool."

"Oh, no, it wouldn't. It would be *terrible*," said Cass.

Twelve

CASS WANTED TO GO STRAIGHT TO MARCEL'S and tell him about the trailer park. But there was only another hour of light before sunset, and Mom didn't want us out in the woods after dark. "It'll wait until tomorrow," she said.

"Maybe I'll go with you," Tim said. I was surprised, but then I figured that he wanted to meet Marcel.

Marcel opened the door the next morning before we even knocked. He looked pleased to see us, even though we'd been there just the day before. "Come in, come in!" We all crowded into the room. "So I meet a new one of yous dis time."

I introduced Tim, and Marcel grasped his hand and shook it. "Now I make some tea or coffee."

"You don't have to bother," Cass said. "We came to tell you something extremely important. Somebody's building a trailer park on Half Moon Bay!"

"Trailer park?" Marcel furrowed his craggy eyebrows.

"Do you know anything about it?"

He shook his head. "Not'ing but swamp in Half Moon Bay." He went over to the stove to put the coffeepot on.

Cass and I told him about the sign. "I called the phone number to find out who it was," she said. "I thought it would be Pelletier, but it was some company called Waterfront Investments. When I started asking questions, they clammed right up. They might talk to an adult, though. Do you know whose land it is?"

"All round Half Moon Bay, dat land is Algonkin land," said Marcel. "Algonkin land, always. De king of England never treaty for it wit Algonkin. White men come and say they bought it. From who? Mississauga, dey say. But dis is not Mississauga land and never was. No big deal, white men say, it belong to some Indian, all the same. Anyway, no problem—plenty land for everybody. Only, pretty soon all de trees are gone. All de animals gone. Pretty soon we gone."

"But if the Algonkins are all gone—" Cass began.

Marcel pointed to himself. "There is still me. My gran'-fadder own dis side, long time. An' I bought that land other side of the bay, ten years ago."

"Well, I don't get it then." Cass frowned. "How can anybody build on it if it's yours?"

"Nobody can." Then he thought a moment. "But somebody for some reason is fixing up the old lake road. Time I go fin' out about that." He didn't seem to be overly concerned, though.

Cass persisted. "It seems like somebody doesn't know it's your land, because they're going right ahead and building on it."

"Don't worry, I look into it," he reassured her. "Jus' some mistake, I t'ink."

"Or maybe they're counting on you not having enough money to go to court to stop them."

Just then the coffee began bubbling and hissing, and Marcel shuffled over to lift it off the stove. He filled our mugs, sweetening the coffee with condensed milk. Cass and I got the jelly glasses this time.

Cass sipped hers. "This is *so* much better than what Mom and Dad make," she said. "What's your secret?"

Marcel grinned. "Boil two, t'ree hours, no more."

I'd brought along the artifacts we'd found in the fields, and it seemed like a good time to show Marcel. He took them from the towel I'd rolled them in and turned each piece in his leathery hands. When he came to the strange stone Tim had found, I asked if it could have been used for grinding corn.

"Maybe." He ran a fingernail around the stone, showing us where a line had been carved into it. "Somebody made this for some reason. To tie some string round, maybe." He examined Hugo's arrowhead and then the other one that Cass found. "Algonkin, these must be."

"Are they different from Iroquois arrows?" I asked.

"No different, probably. But Iroquois get guns pretty soon. Some Algonkin keep using bow and arrow long time after."

"Can you shoot a bow and arrow?" Hugo asked.

"No. Only rifle. Here, now I goin' show you somet'ing." He rose from his chair and went to the cupboard, taking down something wrapped in newspaper.

He handed it to me, and I opened it on my lap—a darkened wedge of iron with one narrow end. It had engraving on it, too, wavy lines and symbols. "Is it—a tomahawk?"

Marcel nodded, pleased by my surprise. "My gran'fadder find it, not twenty yard from this door. Old pine tree was almost dead an' leaning this way. He was chopping it down so it don't fall on his cabin and tear de roof. Crash! This fall from de tree an' jus' miss 'is head."

"The tomahawk fell out of the tree after all that time?" said Cass. "Wow, that's amazing!"

He nodded. "An' I t'ink, 'undred year ago, maybe more, two men fight hand to hand. Round and round dey go. One jumps right for de *tête*. Swish! He miss, and his 'hawk slam into de tree. It sticks an' he scalped for sure, dat one."

Hugo shivered.

"Tree grow an' grow, hundred years, an' that 'hawk

103

grow up de tree with it. An' my gran'fadder come along an' shake it loose, and it almost part 'is hairs for good!"

I passed it to Cass. "It must be really old. It's made of metal, though," she said.

"Indians like white man's iron. Whole lot sharper den stone."

"But—trees don't grow from the bottom," said Tim. It was the first thing he'd said since we came in. "They grow at the top. Wouldn't the tomahawk be at the same height as it was a hundred years ago?"

"Oh, clever, dis one." Marcel winked at him. "Well, maybe I forget what my gran'fadder tell me. Or maybe he stretch de truth jus' a bit."

By this time, we'd all had a look at the tomahawk, and Marcel wrapped it up to put it away.

"That must be worth a lot of money," said Cass. "You could sell it to Mr. Bonnycastle for his collection."

Marcel didn't seem to like the idea. "Not for sale. I got enough money for one old man. An' those people, dey got enough t'ings that don't belong to dem already." He shut the cupboard door firmly. "You goin' keep looking for more?"

"Yes," I said. "But do you know of any good places we could look near here?"

He pulled a wooden match from his shirt pocket and lit his pipe, sucking on it thoughtfully. "What 'bout Half Moon Bay?"

"That's where we were the day we broke into your cabin, remember?" Cass reminded him. "It wasn't any good. It's all overgrown."

"Down de hill, yes, but I mean where de river come out. Once was rendezvous for fur traders, big camp. Every spring people stop an' trade furs on de way to Montreal."

"I thought the camp was down the hill," Cass said.

104

"Some time there, some time one side of de river or de other. After while, too far to go for wood, too much garbage pile up, so dey move. Always de camp was nearby, though. Black robe priests from France build a chapel. Then comes big sickness, like I tole you. Measles, small-pox, somet'ing like that. Nobody comes to dis place no more. Too much sadness. But maybe they leave t'ings behind. Priests say dey can't take dem to heaven." He sucked on his pipe. "So I ask you—" he looked at me "—why you want to dig dem up again?"

"We wouldn't have to *keep* what we found," I said. "We could put everything back where we found it."

"Oh, yeah. Like with fish," said Hugo. "Catch and release."

Marcel considered this. "Maybe, maybe. Or maybe it's better not to fin' t'ings at all? Better to leave dem where they are?"

I had an idea. "If we found stuff that proved that the village and that church and everything were there, it might stop that company from building the trailer park on your land."

"If it's his land, nobody can build on it without his per-mission anyway," Tim pointed out.

"But what about that sign?" Cass looked worried again. "It said Half Moon Bay for sure."

"Some mix-up, I bet," said Marcel. "Now you told me, I fix it. Nobody is building any trailer park on my land, for sure." He looked fierce enough about it this time that Cass nodded, satisfied.

Since we were already most of the way there, we decided to go around to Half Moon Bay. If we could find where the river came out, we might find the spot where Marcel said the main village was. But when we rounded the point in our boat all we could see were water lilies and bulrushes. Cass headed for what she thought was the mouth of the old river.

For the first five minutes the going was easy enough. We used our oars as poles and grabbed any greenery we could to drag the boat along. The rushes squealed in protest as they parted. It was tough, sweaty work.

"What if we get stuck in here?" Hugo asked.

"We'll be okay," said Cass. "Getting out will be easier."

Tim shouted a warning. "Low-flying pterodactyl!" A heron rose into the air right in front of us, flapping its huge wings. It passed a few feet above our heads.

"Dad says there's some endangered bird in here," Cass said, as the heron disappeared from sight. "The least bittern."

Was there a most bittern? I wondered. I couldn't see a thing except an endless green maze. My hands were sore, and insects circled my head. It was like being in the Amazon.

"How much farther?" Hugo whined. "I'm thirsty."

"Drink your water then," Cass ordered. Her own face was beet red. "Still no sign of solid ground. But I think it's getting shallower."

A bit after that we stopped. "Guess this is as far as we go," she said. "We're aground."

"Land, ho!" Hugo shouted and jumped out—and sank slowly up to his middle.

We all shrieked with laughter at his stricken expression. "Don't laugh!" he howled. "Cass said we were on the bottom. It's her fault!"

"What is it with you and water?" she said. "I'm having déjà vu all over again."

I was laughing so hard my eyes were streaming. Poor Hugo struggled to free himself from the muck, bubbles bursting around him. "Get me out of here!" he cried. "It's quicksand! I'm getting sucked under!"

"Your siblings are heartless, leaving you to sink," said Cass. "I'm glad I'm an only child." She leaned out and grabbed his hand. With a loud sucking noise his feet came free, and he grabbed the side of the boat.

"Don't let him in this nice clean boat," Tim said. "He'll get black crud all over everything. You smell like something dead, Hugo."

"What am I supposed to do then?" Hugo wailed, but he managed to crawl up onto a reed clump.

We left the boat and leapfrogged through the cattails and low bushes. Hugo brought up the rear, dripping. When he reached solid ground, he sat on a rock and poured dirty water from his sneakers. "Good thing I did them up today, or I would've lost them." Suddenly he yelped. "Yarggh! Get it off me!"

Now what was the matter? "He's found a bloodsucker, I bet," said Cass.

"Get it off me! Get it off!"

Tim pointed to a shiny black blob on Hugo's ankle. "There's one."

"Too bad we don't have matches," said Cass. "You can burn them off. Or if we'd brought salt, we could pour that on. It dries them up. Hey, there's another one."

"Get them off!" Hugo was frantic.

"Tim, would you please help him," I said.

Tim got out his Swiss Army knife and levered off the bloodsuckers. He chopped them into pieces on a rock. "That's your blood, Hugo. They didn't get much of it."

"You okay, Hugo?" asked Cass.

"Guess so," he mumbled. He pulled his wet shoes on again and followed behind us, squelching.

We walked along a rock outcrop to higher ground.

107

Nothing much was growing there, just scraggy grass and a few sumacs and bushes. Boulders as big as barrels were scattered around—including one the size of a Volkswagen farther back near the trees.

"Do you think this could have been the village?" asked Cass.

"It's flat and dry, and you can see the whole bay," Tim said. "It'd be hard to attack without somebody seeing you coming."

I felt disappointed. I'd been expecting to see something—anything. "I thought Marcel said there was a church, but there's nothing here. Not even any hollows in the ground."

"Well, you know they didn't have basements," said Cass.

"It was hundreds of years ago, Leia," said Tim. "Almost anything would rot away in that time, unless it was stone."

Cass frowned. "What do you mean, hundreds of years?"

"Three hundred, anyway."

"What are you talking about? I got the idea it wasn't that long ago. Like when Marcel was a little boy."

"He said the black robes were here," Tim said. "That means Jesuits, so, like, a *long* time ago."

No wonder there was nothing to see. I tried to remember my school project. There might have been a wall around the camp, but that would have rotted away to nothing. And there'd have been fireplaces—firepits. "If we could find blackened rocks, we'd know where the houses were, because the fires would have been in the middle of them."

We spread out and scanned the ground for a while. Hugo scrambled on top of a boulder. He was still dripping a bit. "I can't see anything. No trailers yet either."

There were no signs of human activity, recent or ancient, around the swamp. But when we walked back toward the trees, we saw right away that the road builders had been there. Beyond the pines it looked like a ravenous monster had devoured everything in its path. Tree branches as big as my arm had been chewed away on both sides of the new gravel road. We stared openmouthed at the mess.

Cass's face was a thundercloud. "That's evil. They must think they're building an extension of the 401!"

"Looks like they're planning on some *big* trailers," said Tim.

Cass winced and stormed back to the site. She didn't say anything, but I could almost see the cogs in her brain turning. "That has me really worried," she said when we finally caught up to her. "I know Marcel says it's his land, but what if the poor old guy can't prove it?"

Tim sat down on one of the big boulders. "Can't prove it because it isn't true?"

She whirled on him. "What do you mean?"

"Just what I said."

Cass glared. "I suppose you still think he's some kind of pervert."

Tim shook his head. "No, I liked him. I thought he was a great old guy. But he is kind of a tall-tale teller. What about that tomahawk story?"

"That was just him being entertaining," Cass said dismissively. "He wouldn't lie about something serious like owning land. You can tell he meant it."

Tim shrugged. "Whatever you say."

"Anyway," she went on, "Leia had a good idea back at the cabin. We need to get serious about finding the old village. Three hundred years is a really long time. If we can prove the village was here, it would show that this place is important. Historically, I mean."

"Marcel said it was an important trading post," I said.

"That's right. So we could get the government to declare it a National Historic Site."

"And you think they'd listen to a bunch of kids?" Tim asked.

"Mr. Bonnycastle will help us. He's a historian. He believes this place should be preserved."

"It might take a long time to find anything," Tim warned.

"We'll start right away. And we'll need to be very organized. We'll do whatever it takes to save this land from trailerparkhood. Right?" Cass fixed her gaze on each of us in turn until we nodded. Even Tim.

We had another good look around the site before we left, and lo and behold, Tim found a blackened rock that could have been near a firepit. "Unless it's just some kind of black fungus," he said. But I felt sure we were on the right track.

Thirteen

⎯⎯⎯⎯⎯⎯⎯⎯⎯ ↘ ⎯⎯⎯⎯⎯⎯⎯⎯⎯

THE NEXT MORNING, Cass wanted to go into the village to buy a shovel. We had three already, but we needed four, and Cass said the only one they had was broken. "Dad says he'll sponsor us to a really heavy-duty one."

Hugo and I were ready to go, but Tim wanted to stay home and work on the boat. He was almost finished. He'd left it in the water overnight, and when he came up from checking it for leaks, he had a big smile on his face. "Dry as a bone."

Hugo and I had helped with the scraping and sanding, but Tim had done the rest himself. He'd caulked every seam and put on four coats of varnish. He'd painted the floorboards, repaired the broken seat and replaced all the hardware. "All I've got left to do is set the mast and rig it," he said. "Cass's dad said he'd help me. We're doing it today."

"At least you won't be able to use the boat as an excuse not to do things with us anymore," Cass gloated.

But Tim didn't need an excuse—and Cass didn't get that there was no rule that said we had to do everything together. She wanted to do everything in a gang, which was funny, seeing she was an only child. Mom said that was probably the reason. She already got plenty of time to herself. Cass didn't understand that with more kids in the family, you had to find space for yourself. I had my books and imagination, and Hugo—well, who knew *what* went on in Hugo's brain? Tim got his space by not saying much and doggedly finishing everything he started. Mom said I should explain that to Cass. But it wasn't always easy to tell Cass things.

Jonathan Marlan brought the *Arrow* around as a model for rigging our boat. We sat on the dock and watched. Tim had his shirt off, and I noticed that his spots were almost gone.

Cass got restless after a while. "Watching guys with rope is about as thrilling as watching paint dry."

"We could play Monopoly," Hugo suggested hopefully. Cass had her own way of playing, which he thought was great. Everybody went in together to buy property for public parkland and we could all land on it for free. Cass also had to be the bank. She pretended to be an ATM and spit bills out of her mouth. She always spit out a few extra for Hugo.

But today Cass wasn't in the mood. She had other things on her mind—like trailer parks and a new road into Half Moon Bay. "We can't wait anymore, Tim. We're going to town without you."

"Good. See if you can get a pick, too," Tim said. "There's a lot of rocks in that ground. I'll put in twelve bucks, Leia, if you cover the rest."

"Can we get a Popsicle at Pelletier's?" Hugo asked.

"Sure," said Cass. "Or a Fudgsicle or a Creamsicle. Anything you want."

"Take the aluminum boat," said Jonathan.

Although Cass never wanted to take the motorboat, I privately preferred it. It might be noisy and polluting, but it sure got you to where you were going a lot faster. And you didn't get your head cracked if the boom came around when you weren't expecting it.

It took about half an hour to get into town by boat. Once we got out onto the main part of the lake, I could see the cliff that we climbed off to the left and the

Bonnycastles' big place away in the distance. We passed a couple of little islands and turned down the second bay on the right. Cass pointed to the village dock where we were headed. Two children in yellow life jackets were fishing from it with long bamboo poles.

"Americans," said Cass. "You can tell by those poles. I don't know where they get them."

The kids watched us tie up the boat. "Where y'all come from?" the bigger kid asked in a Southern accent.

"The other side of the lake," said Cass. "How about you?"

"Fayetteville."

Hugo laughed. "Where's that?"

"North Carolina."

"Well, have a great visit," Cass said. "Keep an eye on our boat, okay? We'll be back soon."

As we started up the track toward the village, Hugo looked back over his shoulder. "They said they're from Faatville!" he said in a loud whisper. "They're not *that* faa-aat."

"I think they said *Fayetteville*, Hugo," I said.

"You're talking just like them."

"Tourists," said Cass. "Well, a few don't hurt. What we don't need is hundreds more."

We'd been into the village plenty of times with Mom, but coming by boat made it seem like a different place. We walked down the main street past the overgrown stone church and the spruced-up white wooden one, past the ramshackle gas station and the bait store. Hugo found a Quebec license plate on the side of the road. He put it in his pack. "I'm saving this for Marcel's totem."

Pelletier's and the hardware store were across from each other. Pelletier's sold everything from bread to straw hats, and the hardware store carried on where Pelletier's left off, with rubber boots and snowshoes.

113

Our first stop was for Popsicles and candy. It was always warm and dim inside Pelletier's, the shelves stacked with dusty groceries and odds and ends. I picked up an exercise book with a speckled blue cover. It seemed like something schoolkids would have used in the olden days. It must have been on the shelf for a long time, too, because it was only seventy-five cents. I bought it.

Hugo was peering into the giant jars of candy along the counter. "I'd stick to Gummis if I were you," Cass told him. "They can't be too old or else they'd be glommed together."

"What about those?" He pointed to a jar of brown cones with pink insides.

"I wouldn't advise it. They've been here as long as I can remember. Probably since the store opened."

When Mrs. Pelletier finished ringing in our purchases, she motioned for us to follow her to a back room. "They always have puppies," explained Cass. Mrs. Pelletier opened the door, and a brown-and-white hound looked up from a box in the corner. Six pups—all of them white with brown and black spots—curled against her flank.

"That's Belle," said Cass. "She's a hunting dog."

"Wish I could have one," said Hugo.

"They are all sold," said Mrs. Pelletier.

"Besides, Hugo, you can't have a dog in an apartment," I said. "It wouldn't be fair."

"And your rabbit probably wouldn't be too happy living with a hunting dog," Cass added.

We lifted the pups one by one out of their box. They squeaked and yawned sleepily. "Aren't they too little to be sold?" I asked.

"They were sold before they were born," Mrs. Pelletier said. "Belle is known as a great hunter. But they won't leave their mother until they are weaned."

Hugo held up the fattest pup. It yawned so wide that I could see the inside of its mouth was spotted, too. Belle stepped out of the box and came to sniff Hugo, then went and lay down again. "Can I take this one outside to play?" Hugo asked. Mrs. Pelletier said that would be all right.

While Hugo sat in front of Pelletier's playing with the pup, Cass and I crossed the street to buy shovels. The hardware store had videos and DVDs, but it was just as gloomy and old-fashioned as Pelletier's. We found the garden tools in the aisle with the chain saws and the moose calls. Cass chose the most expensive shovel with a long handle.

I hefted a pick. "It's seventeen bucks. Does that seem like a good deal?"

"What does Tim want a pick for?"

"To move some of those boulders and see if there's anything underneath."

"He'd never move that huge one in a million years."

"There are lots of others that aren't as big."

Heading to the counter, we noticed some sort of commotion going on between the cashier and two men. "I told you over and over you can't smoke in here, Matt," the woman was saying. "It's against the law. Get outside with that thing." The man moved toward the door with a burning cigarette, grumbling and swearing.

I grabbed Cass's arm. "It's Matt and Lenny!"

"Again? Oh, yeah. I should have recognized the plumbers' butts."

Lenny got his change and went to join his buddy. Cass and I paid and peered out the door to see if the coast was clear. It wasn't. Matt and Lenny had only crossed the street to talk to Mr. Pelletier. We amused ourselves reading the ads for used refrigerators on the store window. Then Cass picked up a copy of *The Beaver*, the local newspaper.

"Now here's something interesting," she said after a minute. "There's a story about the Bonnycastles' break-in. The police are asking anyone who heard a boat on our lake that night to contact them. I guess they haven't caught whoever did it."

I was still watching the men through the window. "Now look who's arrived!"

A silver BMW had pulled up at the curb. Mr. Pelletier wiped his hands on his butcher's apron and walked around to open the driver's door. Out stepped Mrs. Bonnycastle, just like a movie star in dark glasses. Then Paul got out the other side!

He walked quickly into the store while Mrs. Bonnycastle stood under the awning and talked to Mr. Pelletier, Lenny and Matt. They were only about three feet away from Hugo and the puppy. Then Lenny and Matt left in their rattly truck, and Mr. Pelletier and Mrs. Bonnycastle talked for a while longer.

When Paul came back out, he waited around for a bit, unwrapped something and then got in the car. Mrs. Bonnycastle finally joined him and drove off. Paul was staring straight ahead. He was wearing sunglasses, too, so it was hard to tell if he'd seen us, but it didn't seem like he had. Mr. Pelletier went into his store.

"Take that pup back to its mother," Cass called to Hugo as we ventured out of the store. "We're leaving."

"Okay, okay." He carried the little dog inside while we waited for him down the street.

"So were those guys talking to Mr. Pelletier about anything interesting, Hugo?" Cass handed him the shovel to carry. "Could you hear?"

"They were the ones who wrecked Mom's studio, right? They were just talking about some stuff Mr. Pelletier wanted them to do."

116

"Bad business decision," said Cass.

"What about Mrs. Bonnycastle?" I asked. "Did you hear that, too?"

"That's eavesdropping, Leia."

"It's information-gathering," said Cass.

"Huh. Sure I could *hear*. But they were talking French. I didn't understand it very well."

"Hugo, you're in French immersion!" I said.

"Yeah, but we don't talk it like that." He brightened. "It was something about *patates frites* and hot dogs. Maybe it's for Roger's or Anne-Sophie's birthdays."

"Just as long as we don't get invited."

"It's my birthday pretty soon," Hugo said. "Don't anybody forget that."

The American kids weren't at the dock anymore, but our life jackets and paddles were all where we'd left them. We headed toward home. Halfway across the bay, Cass pointed to a white spot out on the blue lake—a sail.

"I bet that's Tim!" I said. And as we turned into our bay, Tim tore by in the *Gull*, its freshly varnished sides glistening, the new sails bright blue and snowy white. As he passed, he gave us a thumbs-up. He looked very happy.

"I thought we were all going to be in on the maiden voyage," Cass shouted at him.

Hugo and I exchanged a glance. She sure didn't know Tim very well.

Fourteen

❧

EMPIRE EXERCISE NOTEBOOK
LINED
75¢

Official Expedition Log of the archeological dig at roposed historical site, Algonkin village and traders' rendezvous.

Official scribe: Leia Jessica Greenway

July 7, This Year of the Millennium: Visit to Marcel Campbell, descendant of Algonkin chief, to report illegal threat to land. Then penetrated swamp to site of old Algonkin village. Blackened stones, likely part of hearth in Algonkin dwelling, discovered by T. Greenway. Also saw hideous new road near site.

July 8: Expedition to village to buy digging implements. Got this book at Pelletier's, almost antique. Also Gummi Feet and Gummi Worms and antique banana Popsicles. Mr. Pelletier spotted talking to evil unhandymen Matt and Lenny. Then Mrs. Bonnycastle appeared (also Paul!). Hugo overheard talk of hot dogs. A plot? Tim launched the *Gull* at long last! Woo-hoo!

I expected to start digging the next day, but as I was eating breakfast, Cass turned up with a change of plans. She sat at the table and accepted a slice of toast with peanut butter and grape jelly. "I've decided we need to go back to the Bonnycastles to get information on Algonkins from the library." She brushed crumbs off her shirt and reached for another half-slice of toast. "Hey, this combination is great."

"But we *have* to get digging, Cass," I said. Three days had passed since we'd learned about the trailer park.

"Yeah, but we need to be properly organized. I want to know the kinds of things we're searching for. Also," she added, "it's the weekend, and I'm hoping Mr. Bonnycastle will be there. It'd be great to have him backing us up."

"Should we call and see if it's okay to go over?"

"We don't need to bother. Mrs. Bonnycastle said to come any time." She turned to Tim, who was reading a yachting magazine while he ate. "I suppose you're not coming. You're probably still contagious, right? Or you have to work on the boat?"

Tim looked up. "The boat's done. Maybe I'll come."

Cass pretended she was falling off the bench in astonishment, but I wasn't surprised. Hugo and I had told him about the Bonnycastles' place and I knew he wanted to see it for himself.

"So, let's go. Where's Hugo?" Cass asked.

"Feeding his crusts to a red squirrel."

"What's he feeding red squirrels for? They eat birds' eggs."

Hugo appeared at the screen door. "They do?" He looked horrified.

"Yeah." Then she grinned. "But so do people. Get your life jacket."

Mom was on the porch looking across the lake. "I don't think it's a good idea to go right now, Cass. That sky is rather ominous."

119

"The weather report says it's clearing," Cass assured her.

"You'd better take the cell phone, in case you get into trouble."

Cass hated cell phones—of course. "If we get into trouble, it'll be because we've sunk," she told Mom. "So the cell phone will be sunk, too. Otherwise, we won't need it."

"Oh, for heaven's sake," said Mom.

As we prepared to push off in the aluminum boat, Cass looked up at the sky. "Maybe it is going to rain. We could ask Dad to drive us. But then he'd forget to pick us up later, and we could be stuck there for ages."

By the time we were out of our bay, dark thunderclouds were piling up above the hills. In the bright sunlight, they were almost navy blue. "We'd better turn back," Tim shouted above the motor.

"It'll pass," Cass insisted. But a minute later the sun disappeared. The temperature dropped several degrees. Black ripples tore across the water, then churned into little waves that raced down the lake. In the bow Hugo yelled every time he got hit with spray.

Cass slowed the boat to turn into a big wave, then speeded up as we coasted down the other side. She was grinning. "Yippee!"

It *was* kind of thrilling, and the water wasn't cold. But then lightning flashed and thunder rumbled. I peered ahead, hoping to see the Bonnycastles' many chimneys. "We shouldn't be out in this," Tim said.

"We'll get there before it hits," Cass said. "We're not getting rained on yet."

The clouds burst as we reached the Bonnycastles' cove. The rain was mixed with tiny ice pellets that stung our faces. We tried to tie the boat up, but the waves banged it against the dock.

120

"We can't leave the boat here. It's getting bashed around," shouted Tim.

"Put it under cover." Paul stood at the side door of the boathouse. "There's plenty of room." He ducked inside, and a moment later the door rolled up.

The boathouse was huge, with hardly anything in it except a launch and a green canoe hung in a cradle above the water. As Cass and I walked our boat around, Paul put out bumpers. He took the stern rope from me and tied it to a ring. "You picked a bad day to be out."

"We were just ahead of the storm. But it was a bit scary," I admitted.

Hugo wanted to tie the bowline himself. "I got a special knot I invented," he told Paul. He made a long chain of spiderwebby loops, then looked up. "Where'd he go?"

"He couldn't wait forever," said Cass. "Come on, before it really starts coming down."

Hail was already drumming on the boathouse roof. We raced up the path, dodging from tree to tree. At the front door, Cass yanked off her sweatshirt and gave her hair a brisk toweling. "Must look our best to get past the gatekeeper."

The door swung open to reveal a scowling Carmen. Cass gave her a big smile. "Hi, Carmen. Mrs. Bonnycastle said we could come *anytime*."

The housekeeper turned without a word and led us down the echoing hall. Roger and Anne-Sophie were in the playroom watching *Honey, I Shrunk the Kids*.

"Oh, it's you again," said Roger.

"Hi," said Cass. "Your mother told us how much you enjoy us coming around. So we're back."

Two pairs of eyes shifted back to the screen.

"Is your dad here?"

Roger shook his head.

"Blast. Too bad. Well, want to play cards?" Cass asked. "Pig? Russian pinochle? Gin?"

Something flickered on Anne-Sophie's face. "Go Fish?" Tim groaned.

"Okay, great," Cass said. "Let's play in the library, okay?"

"We can't watch videos in there."

"We can't watch videos *and* play cards. Where are the cards?"

Anne-Sophie and Roger followed us reluctantly. The rain was pouring down in sheets now. But once the lights were turned on in the library, the room looked cozy, even with the stern-faced chiefs staring down from the walls. I saw Tim's eyes widen.

Cass dragged him to the shelves, and Hugo and I got trapped into playing the first game of Go Fish. "How come they're not playing?" Anne-Sophie asked suspiciously.

"Go Fish is best with just four," I said.

She prodded Hugo with a sticky finger. "You start."

Meanwhile Cass was flipping through indexes. She stacked books on the table: *Indians of North America, Campfires and Gods, Man in Nature.* "How come so many of these are about American Indians?" she grumbled. "At least half the tribes lived in Canada. And I can't find anything on Algonkins."

"It was Algonkins that lived around here," Roger said, claiming a card from my hand.

I was surprised. "How do you know that?"

"Daddy said."

"Is that right? What else did he say?" I asked.

He shrugged and asked if I had any queens. I had two. He laid down his cards—his third win in a row.

Anne-Sophie shrieked in outrage. "You sure you're not cheating, Roger?" I muttered.

"Why are you so interested in Indians?" he asked.

"I bet you're after treasure," Anne-Sophie smirked. "Like those burglars." She pointed to the light patches on the walls.

"What do you mean, treasure? You mean native artifacts," I said. "We're not interested in treasure. We just want to know where people lived."

"Yeah," said Hugo.

"Did the police find all the stuff that was stolen yet?" Cass asked Roger.

"No. How come you're reading all those books? Why don't you look on the Internet?"

"Because we don't have Internet at the cottage," Cass said. "It's a cottage, not a house. Besides, what we're interested in happened a long, long time ago. You wouldn't find that on the Internet."

"Yes, you would. People post old stuff all the time."

"Yeah? What about this?" She prodded at the page in front of her. "This book is written nearly two hundred years ago. Listen to this bit about the Iroquois." She read it out: "The Iroquois were a noble-appearing honorable people, physically more superiorly endowed than the French, most of the men being closer to six feet in height than five. Their coloring was a smooth pale olive, certainly not tawny, and perhaps lighter than that of men I might meet in the streets of Paris."

She looked up triumphantly. "Cool, eh? Imagine meeting an Iroquois in Paris. Are you trying to tell me you'd find that on the Internet?"

"You could," said Roger.

"Come on," said Anne-Sophie, prodding Hugo again. "It's your turn to deal."

Hugo pushed the cards away. "I'm quitting."

"Actually, I think the others should get a turn," I said. "It's only fair."

123

Cass and Tim reluctantly took our places. "I found the book we want. It has pictures of all kinds of artifacts," Cass said. "Write stuff down, okay, Leia?"

I got some paper out of the wastebasket. The book she meant was a sort of catalog with photographs of arrowheads and grinding tools, clay pipes and pottery. I made some drawings with notes underneath. Some of the pottery in the book had markings like the pieces I'd found in the garden. I also learned that broken pieces of pots were called *shards*.

Hugo was turning pages in a book with black-and-white engravings. He pushed it across to me. "See this, Leia? It shows how to get your tomahawk out of a guy's head if it gets stuck when you're scalping him."

I shut my eyes and pushed it back. In my book I spotted a picture of a stone just like the one Tim found in the field. It had string wound around it. It *was* a grinding stone, like I thought.

There was a tapping of heels in the hallway and Mrs. Bonnycastle appeared, this time in a shiny yellow shirt and floppy pants. "*Bonjour, bonjour!*" she said gaily. "I'm so glad you didn't wait to be invited. And this is a new face—Tim, I think. Yes? Welcome!"

"Thanks," said Tim.

"I see you are looking at my husband's books again."

"And having a card game with Roger and Anne-Sophie," Cass said. "I was wondering when Mr. Bonnycastle is going to be here."

"He is busy, busy." Mrs. Bonnycastle clearly wasn't happy about that. "Traveling here, traveling there. Perhaps next weekend we will see him. But what a terrible storm this is. You must stay until it has passed." It was still thundering and lightning, and on the other side of the French doors rain swept across the lawn.

"Our mother might be worrying," I said. "Maybe I should call her."

"But your mother is an artist—I did not think artists worried! Never mind, I will call her and tell her you are safe." Mrs. Bonnycastle stopped on her way to the door. "Where is Paul? He isn't with you?" She frowned. "He is not in the house. How can he be out in this storm? He never says what he is doing or where he is going. Is he taking drugs? Does he have a broken heart? He tells me nothing. I suppose it is a stage you all will go through."

Anne-Sophie looked indignant. "I won't, Mama!"

"Of course not you, *chéri*." Mrs. Bonnycastle kissed the top of her head.

I came to Paul's defense. "Paul helped us move our boat into the boathouse to get it out of the storm. It was very nice of him."

Mrs. Bonnycastle raised her eyebrows. "That is unusual. Perhaps we are having a positive effect on him after all." Rain lashed the window and she shivered. "I will send Carmen in to light the fire for you."

"I'll light it," Cass said quickly. "No need to bother her."

Mrs. Bonnycastle pursed her lips. "I don't permit the children to touch matches."

"Dad taught me about fire safety. I make all our fires. I'm good at it." Cass took a matchbox from the mantel and struck a flame. "I promise I'll close the screen as soon as it's going."

"Very well. See that you do. I'll go and telephone your parents." Mrs. Bonnycastle swept out of the room.

"I'm starving," Hugo muttered. "Last time there was chips." He sidled over to Cass. "I'm starving," he repeated.

She pulled a battered Snickers bar out of her pack. He ripped off the wrapper and began licking chocolate from the foil. "Thanks!"

By now the fire was burning cheerfully. Anne-Sophie abandoned the game of Go Fish and poked at the wood, making the sparks jump. Cass had to stop her from burning the cards. "You're a real little pyromaniac, aren't you? So, tell us about your cousin," she prompted. "Why's he staying? He doesn't seem too keen on being here."

Anne-Sophie seemed pleased to know something that Cass didn't. "He hasn't anywhere else to go."

"But he wasn't here last year or the year before."

"Nobody else wanted him this summer," said Roger.

"Not even his parents?"

"They moved to the States. He goes to boarding school." Roger made a face. "But he acts like he's a hippie. He says 'Right on' to Mama."

"He wants to eat in his room, but Mama won't let him," Anne-Sophie added. "It's bad manners." She whacked at a log, sending a shower of embers onto the carpet.

Cass stomped out the sparks and confiscated the poker. "I promised your mother we wouldn't burn the place down. So what does Paul do with his time?"

"Just stays in his room."

"Or he goes out in that old—" Roger's voice faded. He turned toward the French doors.

Paul walked in. Water dripped from his lank hair, and his jacket was soaked at the shoulders. He stopped in surprise when he saw us, then groped for the door handle.

He's shy, I thought. "Don't go back out in the rain," I said quickly. "We made a fire. You can dry off in front of it."

He hesitated, then shrugged off his jacket and left it on the door handle, taking his Discman out of his pocket. Headphones on, he crouched on the hearth rug.

Anne-Sophie gathered the cards and began dealing

another round with excruciating slowness. I stole a glance at Paul. He was as close to the fire as a person could get, and he was steaming.

He glanced up and saw me staring at him. He took his headphones off slowly. "You're awfully wet," I blurted out. "Maybe you should go and change."

"I'm okay."

"But there's steam coming off you! Like dry ice," I blundered on. "Like in *Buffy*."

"Yeah, and I'm a vampire."

"I didn't mean that!"

Cass came to my rescue by changing the subject. "Hey, do you know Marcel Campbell?" she asked him. "An old guy with a cabin near Half Moon Bay? Because he knows you."

After a moment Paul nodded.

"That old phoney," scoffed Roger.

Hugo rounded on him. "He is not!"

"Mama calls him that," said Anne-Sophie.

"That's not very nice of her," I said. My face was still burning from when Paul had looked at me.

Tim was reading the notes I'd made for Cass. Suddenly Paul got up and strode over to him. "That's not for you to look at."

"It's my sister's," Tim protested.

"What are you talking about?" Paul grabbed the paper. Tim yanked back. For a moment I thought they were going to fight. There was a ripping sound then, and Tim let go. Paul snatched up the page and stalked out of the room.

Cass broke the silence. "Whoa! That was hostile."

"He took my notes!" I cried. "What did he do that for?"

"You never know what he's going to do," said Roger. He looked at me. "You liked him before, didn't you?

127

Better than us. 'Cause we don't go in boats or swim in the lake."

"I wouldn't say we liked him *better*," said Cass. "But I don't see the point of coming to the lake and staying indoors all the time. You might as well stay in the city."

"There's insects outside." Anne-Sophie screwed up her pudgy face. "And slimy things in the water that come up and bite you."

"Like what?" Hugo asked uneasily.

"Fish don't bite people," said Cass.

"There are frogs," said Roger.

"They don't even have teeth. I guess there are loons," Cass amended. "And dragonfly larvae. And water snakes."

"What about turtles?" said Hugo. "Once I heard a snapping turtle bit off a man's—"

"Hugo," I interrupted.

"Anyway, none of them bother you if you don't bother them," said Cass.

Anne-Sophie stood up and stamped her feet. "Everybody has to play Go Fish. Not just these two, but *everybody*."

Two rounds later, I looked out the window. "The rain's stopped!"

"Free again," trilled Cass, breaking into a run across the wet grass.

I raced after her. "I played Go Fish so many times I'm growing gills. They cheat, too."

"I won two times and Anne-Sophie kicked me under the table," Hugo complained.

"That was me," I confessed. "I was trying to stop you from winning so she didn't throw a fit."

Tim came up behind us. "Remember that piece of paper Paul grabbed?"

"My notes, you mean?" I said. "I don't see what his problem was. I got it out of the wastepaper basket."

"That probably explains it," said Tim. "There was something on the back. Didn't you see?"

"No."

"It was a map of Half Moon Bay."

Cass stopped short. "You're kidding."

"He must have thrown it away, but he didn't want us to see it. It had all these spaces marked off. Something about sixty-four electrical outlets."

It came to me in a flash. "The trailer park!"

"Yeah," said Tim. "And you know what else? It had 'Bonnycastle' written on it: 'Proposed Bonnycastle Development.'"

"You sure?" Cass said. "You didn't get a very long look."

"Long enough. It was drawn by hand. Paul must have done it. He sure didn't want me seeing it."

I was confused. "You think the *Bonnycastles* are building the trailer camp, Tim?"

"That's what the map said."

"*Mrs.* Bonnycastle," said Cass. "Mr. Bonnycastle wouldn't have anything to do with it."

"But it's Marcel's land," I said. "Mrs. Bonnycastle can't build on it."

"She wouldn't care," said Cass. "She calls him an old phoney, remember? She'll build and then hire lawyers to say he's wrong. The poor old guy doesn't have any money to fight her." She started running again. "We've got to go and tell him," she said over her shoulder. "Not tomorrow—right now. This is getting really, really bad."

We took the boat straight to Half Moon Bay. But when we got to Marcel's, he wasn't home. I checked his cupboard, and it was nearly empty—not even any bread. "Maybe he's gone shopping."

Hugo held up a piece of cardboard from the table. "Look what I found."

Marcel had written a message on the back of an old cereal box: MARCEL, HE LIVE HERE. BACK SOON. Just what he said he was going to write.

"The sooner the better," said Cass.

Fifteen

➤

July 10: Fact-finding mission to Bonnycastles takes unexpected turn. T. Greenway discovers plan of trailer park. Mrs. Bonnycastle is building it! Is Paul in on it? Went straight to Marcel's to alert him, but he's gone somewhere. Left note that he'll be back soon.

July 12: Stone (flint?) chips, maybe from making arrowheads, found near fireplace (blackened stone) at site. Marcel still away. Watered his squash and other droopy things.

July 14, Bastille Day: Took day off from digging. Went swimming. Cass's mom here for holiday weekend, brought pizzas, enjoyed by all.

July 15: Copper (?) coin (?)—anyway, flat round thing made of metal. Too corroded to see if any writing on it. Found by T. Greenway near fireplace.

At first I didn't like sailing much, but I was beginning to get the hang of it. Still, it didn't seem to me like an easy way to get places. "It's not about arriving," Cass said, "it's about enjoying yourself on the way. Sort of like life."

But I still worried about tipping over. Then it actually happened. Cass just got the boat right side up again and we climbed back in and bailed it out.

"I meant to tip," she said, water dripping off the end of her nose. "I wanted you to have the experience."

Yeah, right.

The digging was going okay. A book on archeology I'd read at the Bonnycastles talked about "circle digs." Apparently, real archeologists would often dig in circles around objects that might have had some human purpose. So that's what we did around the first blackened rock that Tim found. It worked, too—Tim found a round thing that looked like a coin. We didn't have any acid to clean it with, so we soaked it in a mixture of Coke and vinegar when we got home. Hugo found some pottery chips, too.

Then we found more blackened rocks and started other circle digs. The ground was sandy, but the work was still hot and tiring, and the horseflies drove us crazy.

I had this great idea that we should set up a proper archeological camp with a tent. I figured we could even sleep there sometimes, which would have cut down on all the time we spent going back and forth. Cass thought the plan was brilliant, but Tim squashed it.

"Remember what Marcel said about all the people dying here? Leia would see ghosts in the middle of the night and freak us all out." He was right, and Mom probably wouldn't have let us do it anyway.

There were a couple of rainy days when we didn't get over there at all. The next time we did, Hugo found a piece of orange tape. He came over to where we were digging, trailing it behind him. "What do you think this is?"

Tim knew. "Surveyor's tape."

Cass immediately panicked. "They must be getting ready to build! Sixty-four electrical outlets—and we still haven't told Marcel! Where could he be?"

"Probably gone hunting," Tim said. "Or whatever it is he does."

"He told us he was going to check into what was going on. I hope he's okay."

"Maybe Mrs. Bonnycastle knocked him off," said Hugo.

"Things like that don't happen in real life," I said.

Cass frowned. "Don't be so sure."

Sixteen

Official Expedition Log

July 18: Suspicious piece of orange tape—non-aboriginal in nature, eight feet long—found by H. Greenway. Fear this means trailer-camp construction starting. No Marcel. Watered his garden again.

July 19: Rain at night. Cleared by morning, but too soggy to dig. Swam. Water lovely.

July 20: Continued circle digs. Found many small pieces of pottery, brownish clay with designs similar to that found in Greenway carrot patch and Duffault field. (STILL no Marcel.)

July 21: HOT HOT HOT. Giant 1,000-year-old bullfrog named Roger found by Hugo. Possibly heard a least bittern. Had sailing competition on way home. *Gull* sailed by T. and L. Greenway victorious! Swam.

"Stupid sunfish will eat anything." Cass dropped bits of stick off our dock into the water as we dried off in the sun. "See? The silly things are swallowing wood! Hugo, run up to my cottage and get some more bread."

Hugo just screwed up his face and spat into the water. Bits of bubbly spit floated on the surface. Then the water churned in a sunfish feeding frenzy. Disgusting.

"Poor things," I said. "You've poisoned them."

"My spit doesn't poison me, so it won't poison them."

"You sure? Ever kissed anybody?" Cass got to her feet. "I'll make the great sacrifice and get bread."

When she came back, she handed Hugo the bag. "Break it up small and feed it to them just a piece at a time. I'm going to watch." She put her mask on and lay down on the dock again, face in the water. The ends of her long red hair floated on the surface.

After a moment she raised her dripping head. "There are some huge fish down there. You should get your rod," she called to Tim.

"Not worth it." He was still in the water trying to get the last of the dirt off his hands. "They're a lot smaller when you pull them out. Besides, sunfish are mostly bones."

"There's a fish nest right down here," said Cass, pointing. "Some dumb fish built his nest on a public thoroughfare. He's defending his territory against half the population of the lake."

Her face went briefly under again. "Here comes a pickerel. Major battle shaping up!"

A slim, elegant fish approached in the sunlight. I could see the guardian sunfish thrashing his tail over his nest, making jerky movements of threat. The pickerel swam serenely by.

Hugo wanted a turn. Cass passed him the mask. "Sunfish remind me of Anne-Sophie and Roger," he said. "Especially after playing Go Fish."

"Careful what you say," Cass cautioned. "Our life jackets could be bugged. We left them in the boathouse with Paul, remember? Mrs. Bonnycastle's chief spy."

"Paul wouldn't be her spy," I protested. "He doesn't even like her."

135

"But Leia likes him," Hugo teased.

"I don't even know him," I retorted. "So shut up."

"Well, you're way off if you think he's on our side," said Tim. "He went nuts over that map of the trailer park. If it was his, he's in on his aunt's plans."

"And remember, he was with her that day in the village," Cass added.

"He didn't look happy about it, though," I said, thinking of the expression on his face as he stood beside Hugo outside Pelletier's store. "Could you see what he was doing, Hugo?"

"Putting batteries in his Discman," he said promptly.

"See?" I said. "He just got a ride with Mrs. Bonnycastle so he could buy batteries."

"He'd have had to pay big bucks for them at Pelletier's," said Cass. "I hope he disposed of the old ones properly."

A boat zoomed past the dock, pulling two shrieking kids in a giant yellow tube. A minute later the wake hit us. Cass jumped up, dripping. "Creeps! Idiots!" She glared after them. "There's a loon nest along the shore with eggs in it. Those jerks will have washed them out for sure."

"Those eggs must have hatched by now," said Tim. "You've been telling us about them since way back in May."

"But I haven't seen any chicks yet. That's the third boat this morning. I wish we could figure out a way to stop them."

Tim waded over to get his towel off the dock. "Aren't you being a bit selfish?" he said. "I mean, wanting the lake for yourself but not for anybody else? Like it's okay for us to be here, but not other people."

Cass pushed herself up on her elbows, eye to eye with Tim. "Yeah? So?"

"So what's the difference between us and everybody else?"

"That's easy," she said promptly. "We're not hurting anything."

"Because we follow lake rules, right?" said Hugo.

"Yeah, that's right. And because there are not very many of us. Same as with the world—when there were just a few people, things were fine. Now that there are billions, it's wrecking everything. Okay?"

Tim shrugged. "Whatever. I still think it's an excuse for being selfish."

Cass frowned, but before she could reply, the boat pulling the shrieking kids roared past again. "I think that proves my point," she said.

Hugo gazed after them wistfully. "I bet it's fun."

"Maybe if you're *eight*."

"I'm nearly nine. Wouldn't you like to try?"

"Not particularly." But after a minute she added, "Although we did go saucering last year."

"What's saucering?"

"Me and Amy brought one of those old snow-saucer things from home, and Dad pulled us around on it behind the boat. You can't go out very deep, though, because it sinks when you let go."

"Tie a float to it," Tim suggested. "Then it wouldn't sink."

"How come your brother's always so smart?" Cass said to me.

"Have you still got that saucer thing? Can we try it?" Hugo pulled on her arm. "Please, please? Come on, Cass. You never do anything I want to do."

"That's because you're a little geek," she said, ruffling his hair. Then she relented. "Oh, I guess so."

The snow-saucer was collecting dust in the Marlans'

137

boathouse. Cass was a bit heavy for the outboard to pull very fast, but skinny Tim and I were light enough. And, of course, featherweight Hugo was the star. He would have been happy to be dragged around the bay all afternoon.

"He's an addict," I groaned on his fifth turn. Luckily he fell off and got a mouthful of water. We put the saucer away—at least for the day.

Seventeen

WE GOT OVER TO THE SITE so early the next morning the sun hadn't even burned the dew off the grass. As we carried our shovels along the path, I noticed footprints on the sandy soil.

I pointed. "Someone's been here."

Cass came up to look. "Just last night."

"Or this morning," said Tim.

We put down our tools and followed the footprints. One trail went down to the water, but another went back to where we'd been digging. And to the road.

No way the footprints could have belonged to any of us—the person wasn't wearing runners, because the sole was perfectly smooth.

Moccasins.

"Probably a guy," said Cass, fitting her own foot in the print. "It's a bit bigger than mine."

"Wearing moccasins," I said. They all looked at me.

"Must be a ghost then," said Tim. "Indians don't wear moccasins anymore."

Hugo was out near the road, still following the trail. "Hey, there are more," he called out. "There are other footprints here, too."

We hurried over. "They're probably ours."

"No, he's right. These are from bigger feet than ours." Tim had found a muddy patch where the road ended with really clear prints. "These must be a size twelve. And you can actually read the brand name on the others— Northstar. And see, fresh tire tracks, too."

"Our activities are being watched!" Cass said dramatically. "By three spies!"

"Yeah," said Tim. "Bigfoot, Northstar and Moccasin Man."

That turned out to be the high spot of the day, and it wasn't even nine o'clock. By noon all we'd found was a few flint chips. A giant deerfly kept buzzing around my head, even though I was wearing a hat and insect repellant. After driving me nuts for about an hour, the thing had the nerve to land on my face. I slapped it—*ow!*—and spattered fly guts all over my cheek.

Hugo was watching with interest. "Yuck," he said, wrinkling up his face. I had to scrape the guts off with my fingernail.

And that's how it went for the whole frustrating day. Two weeks of hard labor, and we weren't getting anywhere. I was beginning to think the spirits in the place didn't want us to find anything.

Sitting on a boulder in the middle of the dig, I tried for the hundredth time to picture the village with all the people coming and going—tried to imagine me among them, sitting by the fire with my brothers and sisters and cousins, listening to our mothers telling stories. I tried to see the faces around the fire: young mothers with babies, little kids, my friends. Sometimes there was a boy on the other side of the fire, a boy I met on the path when I was carrying water and he was coming back from hunting, pigeons hanging from his belt. None of it did any good, though. I was still sitting in the hot sun, a demonic halo of flies around my head.

Tim stomped past me on his way to the drinking-water supply. "You gone on strike?"

I picked up my shovel again. "I sure want to. We haven't found anything in days."

"Maybe there's nothing more to find."

"There is!" I cried. "I'm sure of it."

"Real archeologists don't find things all the time. It might take years."

"Years!"

Cass downed her tools and came over. "Yeah, and you're all going away to your dad's place in August. But what if Marcel is still missing by the time you go and we haven't proved it's a National Historic Site? What will we do then?"

I had an idea. "We need to get the Indian spirits to help us. We should have a séance."

Cass considered it. "How would that work?" she asked.

I hadn't thought it through yet. "We can, uh, burn candles and sing Algonkin songs. Picture the people who lived here. The main thing is to be in touch with the spirits of this place."

"Do we know any Algonkin songs?" asked Tim. "Besides 'Mighty Gitchi Manitou Sent Angel Choirs Instead,' that is?"

"That's a Christmas carol," Cass said. "And I think it's Huron. But I like the idea."

"Mom won't let us stay over here after dark," said Hugo. "It's one of *her* lake rules."

"The séance doesn't have to be here," I argued. "It can be over on our side. We know that's an Algonkin site, too, from the pottery in our garden."

"Can't have it in the garden," said Hugo. "Mom goes nuts if you even walk on it."

"Your beach would do fine," Cass said. "I'm in. We can have a campfire, with songs and sacrifices. You guys can plan it. I'll bring chips and pop."

"Count me out," said Tim. I'd expected that.

141

The next day Cass and Hugo and I cleared all the dead brush from around the boathouse and dragged it to the beach. According to Cass, cedars and junipers burned fantastically well. At first Mom was thrilled. She said it made a big improvement in the place. Then she saw the huge heap of brush we'd collected. "You can't burn all that!" she cried. "You could set the whole place on fire! Is it even legal? Don't you need a permit for a bonfire?"

"It's only a campfire, Mom," I said. "And it'll be on the beach—practically in the water."

"The wind could carry the sparks back into the trees."

"It's almost always dead calm by dark," Cass said quickly. "I know what we can do, though. Dad has an old charcoal barbecue that we can wheel into the lake to burn things on. Barbecuing isn't illegal, right?"

Mom looked doubtful. "Better check with your parents."

"They'll be okay with it," said Cass. "I've got them brainwashed."

Then Mom started talking about coming along to supervise. "It'll be really buggy," I told her. "Wouldn't you rather stay in the cottage and read? Cass is an expert with fires."

"You'd spoil it, Mom," said Hugo.

"Thanks very much."

"They mean it'll be embarrassing enough without you there," said Tim. "I'll keep you company in the cottage."

"You *have* to be in it, Tim," Cass said, trying once more to change his mind.

"I don't *have* to be in anything."

Cass's barbecue was like a little red spaceship on legs. She and Hugo wheeled it down the path and into the water. Just before dark we loaded it with cedar boughs and crumpled newspaper.

"Can we rub sticks together to light it?" Hugo asked.

"Matches are way quicker." Cass pulled a matchbox from her pocket, took out a match and struck it. The match ignited and she lit the edge of the paper, which caught with a whoosh, crackling and spitting. It was amazing how fast the pile turned into a fiery mass, the sparks flying into the sky. I stepped back, feeling the heat on my face. The branches glowed red in the heart of the fire, burning rapidly to white ashes. We rushed back and forth with more wood.

"It's all going to burn before it even gets dark," Hugo worried.

"We haven't got to the big stuff yet. Anyway, we can always sneak up to your woodpile and get more logs." Cass sloshed around to the other side of the barbecue. "Isn't it uncanny how no matter where you stand near a fire, the smoke gets in your eyes?"

Eventually we fed all the brush into the flames. Once the bigger logs were burning steadily, Cass got down to business. "Right. We need something to sacrifice. Anybody bring a fatted calf? Or what about Hugo's rabbit?"

"That's not funny," said Hugo.

"We brought marshmallows," I interjected, before he could get himself all worked up.

Hugo hugged the bag tightly. "You're not sacrificing these either, Cass."

"Hand 'em over, kid. If you won't contribute a few lousy marshmallows, why should the spirits reveal their secrets?"

Grudgingly Hugo counted out a dozen marshmal-lows—four apiece. "Toss them into the flames," Cass directed. "Say, 'Sweet gifts for the manitous!'"

We said the words and took turns throwing on

marshmallows one by one, watching as they browned, melted and blackened. The burning sugar smelled great.

"Just the way I like them," Hugo said sadly, staring into the coals.

"Good," said Cass. "You have to give the gods something you value. Okay, Leia, what happens next?"

I hadn't been able to plan much of a ceremony. I didn't have any information at the cottage about native people, except for an old book of poems that used to be Gran's. I didn't even know what kinds of gods the Algonkins had before priests converted them to Christianity. I asked Cass if she knew.

"Manitous," said she promptly. "They believed there were manitous in everything. The lake has a manitou, and so does the sky, and so does the fire, and so do birds and animals and bees. And they're listening all the time, Hugo, so be careful what you say."

"Do they know English?" he asked.

"Sure. Spirits are all-knowing."

"Are there manitous in this beach?"

"In everything."

"In the air?"

"Yes."

"In wood? Even after it's been cut up?" Hugo persisted. "If you had a manitou in a tree and you cut the tree up, would it go into just one board or in all the boards?"

"Shut up, you two, you're hurting my head," I said. "We're supposed to be having a séance here, not a question period. I'll start. I'm reading some poems."

We settled on the sand, which still felt a bit warm from the sun. Cass opened a bag of corn chips and passed it around. The evening was calm, just as she had forecast, the lake like glass. I picked up my book and flicked on my flashlight.

144

"This first one's sort of depressing. It's about a beautiful Indian girl who becomes a white trader's wife. He gets tired of her, so she goes back to her people and they punish her for going off with such a bad person."

The ending was especially mournful:

Keejigo came no more to the camps of her people;
Only the midnight moon knew where she felt her way,
Only the leaves of autumn, the snows of winter,
Knew where she lay.

Cass snorted. "You mean she *died* because some rotten white guy broke her heart? She should have led *him* into the woods and left him there. But otherwise it was good," she added. "Read another."

I had one marked about a headless Indian spirit. It was my favorite, very strange and spooky, called "Powassan's Drum." I didn't exactly understand it. The author's name was Duncan Campbell Scott, so long and proper-sounding that it surprised me his poem was so gruesome. It had the line I'd thought of that night down on the dock when I saw the ghostly canoe: *"The Indian fixed like bronze, Trails his severed head through the dead water by the hair."*

Cass shivered when I finished. "Spooky."

"I don't understand it," Hugo complained.

"It's something about a storm coming," I said. "A force that will destroy everything."

"White people, it probably means." Cass got up and put more big branches on the barbecue. The fire flared, sending fresh showers of sparks into the sky. "Okay, more."

The next thing I had was a story about a man named Pierre Cadieu. "This might have happened somewhere near here, even. The story has French missionaries in it, and Pierre Cadieu might be part Indian."

145

I partly read it and partly told it. Pierre had an Algonkin wife, and they came down the Lievre River in the spring to meet up with other people and buy furs. They always stopped at a village camp that sounded a lot like ours, except it was near some rapids. One year they'd just met their friends when an Iroquois war party snuck up on them to steal their furs. Pierre rushed past the Iroquois so they'd run after him and let the others get away. The Algonkins jumped in their canoes and paddled as fast as they could toward Montreal.

"Pierre's wife wanted to go back for him, but the others said that the Iroquois would kill them. If Pierre was alive, they said, he'd find them."

"Did he get away?" Hugo asked anxiously.

"He did, but he was wounded. He walked nearly all the way to Montreal, but then he died. When they found him, they discovered that he'd written the whole story out on birch bark—with his own blood. But he died a hero."

"I don't like that ending."

"Is it true?" Cass asked.

I didn't know, but I thought because of having Pierre Cadieu's name in it, it might be. "I'll look it up when I get home," I said.

Finally, I had a ceremony I'd read about in the Bonnycastles' library. It was actually a ceremony that people had whenever they caught fish, to thank them so they wouldn't get angry and refuse to be caught. "One person would stand up while the other people were eating and apologize to the fish for taking their lives," I explained. "I think they had ceremonies like that for deer and geese and other things, too. But it might have been a Huron custom, not Algonkin."

"Huron's close enough," said Cass.

My idea was to apologize to the spirits of the Algonkins for what our people did and tell them we didn't want to do any more harm. I'd brought a box with the pottery chips in it, and I thought we could all touch them and be in touch with the hands of their makers long ago.

"Sounds good." Cass passed the corn chips around again and took a swig of pop. "You be the speaker and tell the manitous we're sorry, but we need to find artifacts so we can stop Mrs. Bonnycastle from building on their land."

"I don't know what to say."

She sighed. "Do I have to do everything? Okay, I'll talk to the manitous. Just short, though. And no laughing."

She stood up between us and the fire and raised her arms. "O great manitou of the Algonkins and all manitous who hear my voice. We humbly beseech thee to hear our respectful greetings, O manitous of earth and sky and rocks and trees."

At first she mumbled a bit, but as she began to think of things to say, her voice got clearer. "Great and many manitous, we apologize for the great and many offenses our people did against you, and anything we have done by mistake. Please lead us to where the great Algonkin people of old laid down their things, their bows and arrows and their spears and wampum.

"O great and many manitous, we will treat them with all due respect and offer further sacrifices to your great selves. O great manitous, we are heartily sorry for our sins against you, but it is not we who seek to desecrate your holy places with a trailer park and sixty-four electrical outlets. We love this earth and the water and sky and rocks and trees. We wish to do homage to your great names.

"So be it. And now we will be quiet, and O great and many manitous, speak to our willing thoughts, amen." She lowered her arms and sank to the sand.

147

"What do we do now?" Hugo whispered loudly.

I put the box of pottery shards where we could all reach it and took off the lid. "We should all stick our hands in and touch the pottery. Then we should empty our minds of all other thoughts. Just picture the village. Maybe we'll get a vision of the right place to dig."

Our hands bumped in the dark before we got sorted out. I ran my fingertip over the etchings on the surface of a shard. For a few minutes all I could hear was Hugo and Cass breathing and branches crackling in the barbecue. I imagined the ground where we'd been digging, flat and bare. I couldn't see anything except for the scattered boulders. Then I opened my eyes and gazed up into the inky blue sky. A tiny point of light winked at me: the first star. Another danced at the edge of my vision. Then another.

It was like the manitous were signaling. My scalp prickled.

"Fireflies are out," Cass murmured.

Just fireflies. Not manitous. "I got one up my nose," Hugo complained, and blew it out noisily.

A twig snapped near the boathouse. "What was that?" I sat up, peering into the dark.

A flashlight beam swept us. "Any contact from the spirit world yet?" It was Tim.

Cass jumped up. "Trying to sneak up on us, eh? I thought you didn't want anything to do with our séance."

"Mom sent me down to see if everything was okay. Your fire's almost out."

"We need more wood." Cass threw the last of the juniper on the barbecue. It exploded over the glowing coals, fiery manitous taking flight from every needle.

"There's a rotten ladder against the boathouse," said Tim. "You could burn that." He and Hugo went to get it. Tim waded into the shallow water and they balanced the ladder across the barbecue. Cass and I gathered handfuls of twigs and leaves. Pretty soon the section of the ladder that was in the middle of the fire started smoking. It caught, and the dry wood blazed.

"That's more like a proper Indian campfire," said Tim. Then he started making a woo-woo-woo sound with his hand against his mouth. Hugo joined in, and they both splashed in the water around the fire, whooping.

"Cut it out!" Cass said in disgust. "We're trying to get in touch with the spirits, not go on the warpath."

Tim only deepened his voice and began chanting: "Houma-houma-houma-houma!" Hugo followed him, grunting like a bear.

Cass raised her voice. "That's ignorant. Cut it out!" When they paid no attention, she fumbled around in the dark for her shoes. "Trust guys to turn things into a circus. I'm going home."

"Cass, don't," I cried.

"Forget it, Leia. See you in the morning."

After she left, Tim and Hugo finally wound down. "That wasn't fair," I said angrily to Tim. "You didn't contribute anything, and then you had to go and spoil it. Cass is really mad."

"I contributed the ladder. Anyway, who cares if Cass is mad? Can't she take a joke?"

"It wasn't supposed to be funny!" I shouted. "It was supposed to be serious!"

Suddenly the two ends of the ladder collapsed into the water with a hiss. Smoke and steam filled the air. Tim tried to rescue the smoldering pieces without burning himself, but the water extinguished the glowing coals, leaving us in the dark.

Hugo started shouting. "Look up! What's happening to the sky? Look up!"

149

The new moon was as thin and sharp as a fingernail clipping. The sky, arched above us like a giant black bowl, seemed to be moving. It wasn't the clouds, because there weren't any. The longer we gazed, the more distinct the movement became, flowing up from the horizon in pulsing greenish waves, lapping the stars.

"Gotta be northern lights," said Tim. "I've never seen them before."

Neither had I. I shivered.

I hadn't really expected the heavens to reply.

Eighteen

————————— ➤ —————————

THE HEAVENS MIGHT HAVE ANSWERED, but the earth wasn't giving up a lot of secrets. Every day we found more pottery chips and bits of animal bone, but that was about it. I couldn't stop thinking about our trip to Port Hope. We only had two weeks left.

On Hugo's birthday, July 28, we took the morning off and went sailing, but we still got in three good hours of digging in the afternoon. I found a metal button and Cass found a nail.

While the rest of us were packing up to go, Tim was still working away at a boulder. He was leaning with all his weight on the pick handle, trying to lever the big rock out of the ground. The veins on his arms stood out, and sweat trickled down his bare chest.

"Come on, Tim," I called. "If we're not back in time for Hugo's birthday dinner, Mom's gonna kill us."

Tim ignored me. His arms shook with effort as he raised the rock a fraction of an inch.

I squatted down and managed to peer into the space just before the rock rolled back into the ground with a thud.

"Did you see anything?"

"Nope."

He heaved again. "What about now?"

"Nothing." What was I supposed to be seeing? But wait...what was that? Not earth or roots, but a sort of flap. "Oh, Tim, maybe there *is* something there."

151

"Well, help me then!"

I grabbed the pick handle right below Tim's hands and leaned on it. At that exact moment it broke, sending a shock like fire up my arms. We both fell backward and the rock settled in place again. Tim muttered some words he saved for special occasions.

Hugo and Cass came running back from the canoe. "You guys okay?"

"We broke the pick." Tim grimaced.

"Never mind. We can buy a new handle."

"That'll take too long. There was something under there, and I want to get it now."

"What was it?"

"I didn't see it. Leia did."

"I don't know *what* it was," I said. "It might have been leather."

Cass walked around the rock. It was on uneven ground, and the other side was much more exposed. "Why didn't you dig around this side? I'll get a shovel."

"It's past five-thirty," I said.

"Six, actually."

"We said we'd be back by six! Let's get going." Mom didn't usually make a big deal about when we turned up, but tonight she'd set a time.

"Yeah, it's my birthday," said Hugo indignantly. He'd been looking forward all day to opening his presents.

"What's half an hour?" Tim said, but he was totally outvoted. If there was something under that rock, it would just have to wait.

I had a bad feeling as we walked up the path to our cottage. Hugo threw open the screen door. "The birthday boy's here!"

Mom was reading in front of the window. She marked her place on the page with her finger. "It's about time."

"Sorry we're late, Mom," I said. "But we might have found something important."

"More important than your brother's birthday? More important than a promise to me?"

"It wasn't actually a promise," Tim pointed out.

She stood up angrily.

"Okay, okay," he said hastily. "It was my fault. They kept telling me to come. I didn't think we had to be home *exactly* at six."

"Obviously not." Her eye twitched—a bad sign. "Obviously it meant nothing to you that I've been cooking all day to make a special Indian feast. Wild rice and beans and squash. I even ordered pheasants specially from Pelletier's. I don't know why I bothered. The birds are all shriveled, poor little things. I should have just boiled a package of hot dogs."

"Pheasants? That's an *incredible* surprise, Mom," I said.

"I thought so." She softened a little. "Go and get cleaned up. Where's Cass?"

"Is she invited?" I wiped my face on a dishtowel.

"Of course! It's Hugo's birthday! Jonathan and I made arrangements for her to stay the night. He had to go to Montreal to pick up Naomi, and they won't be back until tomorrow. Oh, there you are, Cass."

Cass edged open the screen door and backed in with a big box in her arms. "Dad's note said to come over."

"By six o'clock," Mom said. "The birthday dinner is in the oven. It's ruined. I ate mine already—when it was *supposed* to be eaten."

Cass caught my eye. "Yikes," she mouthed.

We got our plates from the oven and took them out to the screened porch. Mom had even covered the table with a native-looking blanket. That made me feel even worse.

The pheasants nestled all golden on the wild rice. They

153

smelled fantastic, although they were a bit naked and wrinkled. Cass winced at the sight of hers, but she just slid it onto Tim's plate and started in on her squash. "I'm so hungry my stomach thought my throat was cut." She lowered her voice. "She's pissed off, right?"

I nodded.

"This is *amazingly* delicious," Cass said loudly.

"It's an Indian meal," Hugo said. "Mom thought of it all by herself."

"Too bad they ate squash," said Tim, flipping his onto Cass's plate. "I never did see the point of it."

Everybody kept talking about how good the meal was, and Mom's mood gradually improved. She brought out a cake—cornmeal with maple icing—that had nine candles burning on top. Hugo made a wish and blew them out.

He was itching to open his presents. We'd bought them ages ago in Toronto, and I'd almost forgotten what I'd gotten him—a big stack of Marvel comics and a leopard-skin collar for Rover. Tim gave him a new game for his Game Boy.

"When I blew out my candles, I wished for an Xbox, so maybe I'll get that, too," Hugo said happily. "And Mom's taking me to the skateboard park in Pembroke."

Cass pushed her parcel over. "Sorry about the newspaper wrapping, dude."

Hugo ripped it off. Inside the box were more newspaper packages. He opened one and his face lit up. "Hey, a little baby skull!"

"It's my old animal skull collection," said Cass. "I was thinking and thinking about what to give you. I hope you like it."

"Cool," Hugo said reverently. He unwrapped another.

"Those are both squirrels," she told him. "But there are mice and birds and a muskrat. A turtle, even. And a rabbit."

154

"Don't let Rover see that," said Tim. "It'll upset her."

"Where did you get them all, Cass?" Mom asked.

"Most I just found, ages ago. People gave me some, too. Some were already cleaned, but with others I had to boil off the flesh."

"Well, it's very generous of you to give them to Hugo." Mom picked up a tiny bird skull and turned it in her hands. "I'd like to paint them."

That's when Tim decided to say that he might get the Marlans' crowbar and go back to see what was under that rock before it got too dark.

"You will not!" Mom exploded. "You're going to stay here and be head dishwasher. You're not going out tonight and you're not going over to that place for the rest of the week. Consider yourself grounded. I wish you'd remember you're still getting over a serious illness. You're supposed to be using these holidays to rest. I don't know why you always have to go at things like a madman. You're a bag of bones. When your father sees you, he'll think I've been running a forced labor camp!"

Tim rolled his eyes and went to fill the sink with hot water. The rest of us carried in the plates. "She'll relent," he muttered. "She always does."

But she didn't. No one got out of her sight all evening. By eleven it was lights out and the cottage was silent.

I don't know how long I'd been asleep when something woke me. A small, distinct noise—the clunk of the back door. I sat up and looked across at the cot where Cass was sleeping. She was still there, a mound in the blankets.

Rolling out of my covers, I picked up my clothes from the chair. My fingers closed on the flashlight on the bureau. I padded down the hall, stopping outside the boys' room. Hugo turned in the top bunk. It was too dark to see anything in the shadows below, but only one person was breathing in the room.

Tim had gone out.

I tiptoed to the bathroom, every step taking me farther out of earshot of Mom's room. I pulled on my clothes and slipped out the back door.

Once outside, I switched on the flashlight. Down at the boathouse I flicked the beam around. The boat was tied where we'd left it. I pushed on the boathouse door. "Tim?" The light swept over old paint cans, oars and masts in the rafters. No Tim. So where had he gone?

Back to the site. In Cass's canoe.

I scrambled back up the path, taking the fork to Marlans'. Tim had at least a five-minute start. He could be out on the lake already.

I heard a thump. Something heavy was being dragged over the rocks. I started running, then halted, my heart pounding. What if it wasn't Tim? What if someone was stealing Cass's canoe?

"Ow!" Tim's muffled voice. His face in the beam of my flashlight was alarmed.

"It's me. Leia."

"What are you doing here?" he growled.

"What are *you* doing here?" I whispered back. "You're going over to the site, aren't you?"

When he didn't answer, I said, "I'm going with you."

"Uh-uh. Mom would kill us."

"You're not going by yourself. I won't let you. I'll go and tell Mom. Anyway, it'll be faster with two paddling."

Tim knew when he was beaten. "Okay, come on."

Nineteen

THE MOON WAS GETTING FULLER, enough to light our way. It hung above the hills like half a lumpy grapefruit. We paddled the same way we'd gone every day for weeks, but it felt weird to be doing it in the middle of the night.

And dangerous. What if we tipped? At least it was a warm night. I was wearing a life jacket and so was Tim. We could swim to shore. We had a waterproof flashlight and a whistle. We were following lake rules.

The water was alive. All around us fish jumped at insects on the surface. A beaver or muskrat splashed near the shore. The bullfrogs grew louder and louder as we rounded the point and turned toward the swamp. Then the croaking stopped. We moved across the bay in eerie stillness.

Tim stopped paddling. "Did you hear something?"

"Like what?"

"Like glass breaking. Sort of like a bottle smashing."

"I didn't hear anything."

We drifted, ears straining. A tiny breeze rattled the aspen leaves. Tim started paddling again. Out of the corner of my eye I thought I saw a dark shape pull away from the lake edge. A swift shadow traveled across the water. Then it was gone. A few thin wisps of cloud crossed the face of the moon. Maybe it was just a trick of the light.

The canoe slipped into the channel we'd made with all our comings and goings. We were well into the reeds before we dared to speak. "You see that?" Tim asked in a low voice.

So I hadn't imagined it. "I think so. What was it?" I whispered back.

"It was going way too fast for an animal."

Remember my ghost paddler, I wanted to say.

"Are you scared?" Tim asked.

"A bit." I hoped I sounded braver than I felt.

"We could turn around and go home. But we're here now, right? We might as well have a look. Especially since I'm grounded until Monday."

We left the canoe in the usual spot and carried the tools over the trampled reeds. Dew-soaked grass slapped against our ankles. "We'll just check it out and take off," he promised. "I couldn't get to sleep. I kept wondering what it was you saw under that rock."

"Cass will never forgive us for coming back without her. Hugo will be furious."

Tim didn't answer. Then I heard a sort of *thwump*.

I whirled, hair standing on end. No Tim. He was simply gone. Frantically I swept the ground with the flashlight. The batteries were so weak I could hardly see more than a few yards. "Tim!"

I just made out his outline as he rose from a clump of reeds. "I tripped." He picked up his crowbar. "Listen to us, whispering. Like anybody's going to hear." He raised his voice to normal. "There's nobody for miles."

I pointed with the flashlight. "There's your rock." The feeble orange beam barely illuminated it. "This thing is dying."

"I can see fine without it."

I could, too. I watched while he poked under the rock with the shovel. "Cass said you should try from the other side."

He grunted, then worked at the exposed edge. "She's right." He sounded surprised. "It's a lot easier. I might not even need the crowbar." Throwing aside the shovel, he felt around under the rock. "There *is* something here! I touched it!"

We scrabbled at the dirt with our hands. "It's not leather. More like cloth—a cloth package."

"Don't pull too hard or you'll rip it. It'll be rotten." Tim's voice rose. "Got it!"

And, like a cork out of a bottle, whatever it was came free.

We ran around for a minute high-fiving each other and laughing. "I knew there was something there. I told you!"

"Cass is going to be so steamed that she wasn't here! What do you think it is?" I tried using the flashlight again but couldn't get a flicker.

"Not a body, I hope."

"Ha, ha." It wasn't big enough for that.

Just as Tim bent to open it, a branch snapped in the bulrushes. We froze. Twigs crackled. "Something's out there, Tim!" Heart in my mouth, I waited for whatever it was to charge at us. But only small things rustled in the darkness, soft sounds of animals going about their business.

Tim let out his breath. "We're just hyped up."

In the pines out by the road a faint flicker of moonlight reflected on something shiny. "What's that?" I asked.

"Where?"

Leaving the bundle on the ground, we crept closer. Something was definitely there—something large and solid that hadn't been there when we left the site at six o'clock.

I tried to make it out in the darkness. "It's a truck!" How did it get here? And what was all that stuff on the back?

"A well-drilling truck." Tim walked toward it. "Somebody must have brought it around after we left."

"Drilling for what? Oil?"

He laughed. "No, water." He pointed up at the cab over the chrome teeth of the radiator. "Remember when I thought I heard glass breaking?"

In the center of the windshield was a gaping hole. Glass fragments glittered on the engine hood. "Somebody heaved a rock through it."

Filled with a sudden dreadful premonition, we ran back to where we'd left the bundle. My heart was pounding—I was sure it would be gone. But the bundle was still there. Tim gathered it up. "Let's get out of here," he said. "This place is giving me the creeps." We hurried to the canoe—or at least to where we had left it.

The canoe was gone.

Tim groaned. "Oh, man, this night just goes on and on. It's like some kind of crazy dream." Stumbling and staggering over the rush clumps, we gazed down the channel.

"There it is." Carried on the faint current of the old river, the boat was drifting on the moonlit water.

Tim swore. "I didn't pull it up far enough." He thrust the bundle into my arms and began stripping off his T-shirt and jeans. "No point in both of us getting wet."

"But your chicken pox!"

"I'm over that." I stood clutching the heavy sack as Tim waded out into the black water. I could smell swamp gas rising from the rotten leaves on the bottom. A minute later the reeds blocked him from view. I imagined bloodsuckers, eels, snapping turtles.

What if he didn't come back?

Twenty

⟶

"TIM! TIM!" I SCREAMED.

No answer.

Tim was drowned and I was helpless. I sat on the damp grass and cried like my heart would burst.

Someone thumped me with a pillow. "Shu' up, Lee. S'early. You're havin' a nightmare."

I sat up. Cass was squinting at me from the cot across my room. Out the window the sky was pearl gray. Tim wasn't lost in the blackness at the bottom of the bay, and I was safe and dry in my own bed.

I flopped back down on the pillow, my heart thudding. A nightmare, Cass said. Had I dreamed the whole thing? No. Tim really *did* swim out and catch the canoe— and we made it home without being drowned or murdered.

And then I remembered what we'd seen inside the bundle, glimpsed by the flickering light of a match.

It was nearly nine by the time everyone got up. Mom had long since gone out to her studio. Tim was the last to the table. I was so happy to see him, rumpled and yawning and definitely alive. He filled a bowl with corn flakes and reached for the blueberries. "Hey, Hugo," he said, "you sleep okay?"

"Yep," Hugo said, shoveling in cereal.

"How about you, Cass?"

"On that cot? Every bone in my body aches." She frowned at him suspiciously. "Why?"

"Just checking." He piled on more blueberries. "Me and Leia had major insomnia."

"Okay, dude, you're being really weird. What's up?"

"We'll tell you," Tim said mysteriously. "But first you and Hugo have to swear a vow of secrecy."

Cass bristled. "What the heck is this all about?"

"Say, 'I swear by the ancient oath of Lake Wasamak to remain silent about what is to be revealed.'"

"Even under torture," I added. "And you have to promise not to get mad."

"Don't you trust us?" Hugo scowled.

We waited. Cass and Hugo swore the oath.

As Tim began relating the events of the previous night, Cass's eyes widened. "Hold on a minute here. You went without me?"

"You swore you wouldn't get mad," I reminded her. "Anyway, if we'd woken you up, Mom would have heard."

"I didn't even want Leia to come," Tim said. "But I might not have made it back alive if she hadn't."

"Go on."

Tim and I told the story between us. Cass kept interrupting. "You took my canoe and you didn't take me? You've got a lot of nerve!" She was mad all right, but when we got to the part about the bundle under the rock, she and Hugo got really excited. "And you say there was a truck?" she said incredulously. "How did that get there?"

"A well-drilling truck," I said.

"With a smashed window," Tim added. "I heard it break. Somebody did it just before we got there."

"Man, this is confusing."

Hugo shuddered at the part about Tim's midnight swim. "Yuk. Did you get bloodsuckers all over you?"

"I was moving way too fast. Anyway, we got the sack into the canoe and paddled home like we had seventy horsepower on the back."

"How could the canoe just float away?" asked Cass. "There were no waves."

"We must not have pulled it up far enough," said Tim. "There's a bit of a current where the old river drains into the lake."

"Whoever broke the truck window let it go, I bet."

"We thought we saw somebody leaving when we got there," I said, "after Tim heard the glass break."

"But we weren't really sure we'd seen anything," said Tim. "I just figured it was one of Leia's Indian ghosts."

"Where's the bundle?" asked Hugo.

We trooped down to the boathouse, and Tim reached into the rafters where he'd hidden it the night before. He set it carefully on the floor, the rotten wrapping falling open around it.

We all stared at the treasure inside. It was like Christmas morning. I'd had a quick look the night before, but it was even better in the full light of day. Tim lifted up strings of tiny beads. Some were white, some purple, some black. "That's wampum," I said reverently. "I've never seen it before. In the flesh, I mean."

A bit of tattered leather that was still barely a purse held a dozen black coins. Once they must have been shiny silver. Some had a picture of a man's head.

"That could be a king. Or Napoleon," Cass said.

There were two leather bags—a big one and a smaller one, decorated with dyed porcupine quills and more beads. They had shoulder straps, and the leather was dark and stiff as a board with age.

Tim hefted a war club, testing its weight. It was the biggest thing in the bundle, over a foot long, polished smooth with a gnarled knob at one end. "For cracking skulls."

I picked up an arrow lashed to a wooden shaft. The head was flat and wedge-shaped, like the one Hugo found in the fields. Tim drew something from the burlap and clapped it against his face. He leapt at Cass, roaring. She jumped back with a scream. Then Tim turned on Hugo and me.

Hugo squealed, but I stood my ground. "Quit it, Tim!"

He lowered the mask. "There's another, too." The one he had was carved wood, painted brown with red blood trickling down a wrinkled chin. The other was partly straw or corn husk. They both had sunken eyes and big leering mouths.

"I've seen pictures of things like that," Cass said.

"But those aren't Algonkin." I knew that from my school project. "They're Iroquois false faces."

"Maybe they were captured in battle."

Hugo held the wooden mask to his face and stuck his fingers out the eyeholes. "It's got real Indian hair on it. Can we show Mom?" he asked.

We all looked at each other. "Not right yet," Tim said. "Wait until we go over to the site again. I told her last night I wanted to look for something under a rock, but officially I'm grounded."

Cass shook her head. "I still can't believe you went without me. In my canoe."

"Yeah, I'm really sorry," said Tim. "You could have swam out after it instead of me."

Cass shot him a dirty look. "Anyway, it was worth it," she said. "This stuff has got to be worth a fortune. So what do we do with it?"

"Sell it on eBay? What do you mean, *do* with it?" Tim asked.

She folded her arms. "I mean this is a really big discovery. It's not just worth a pile of money—it's *very* important. It proves the site is significant. It's what we were hoping we'd find, only a hundred times better! You guys are heroes."

"What do *you* think we should do?" I asked her.

"The situation's urgent. That well-drilling truck means they're starting work on the trailer park. And we *still* can't find Marcel. I think..." She paused for a moment. "I think we should go to the media. Tell them what we found. It proves the land should be a National Historic Site, not a trailer park."

"Who do we call?" asked Tim. "The CBC or something?"

"And newspapers, like the Montreal *Gazette* and *The Globe and Mail*."

Tim looked skeptical. "Who's going to pay attention to some kids in a hick place nobody's ever heard of? You think they'd send a reporter way up here?"

Cass frowned. Tim had a point. "Well, okay. Let's start by calling *The Beaver* and go from there."

"Just be sure you omit the little detail about me and Leia going out last night. You're sworn to secrecy, remember? Mom doesn't need to know."

"Or you'll get grounded even worse, Tim," Hugo said. "Until you're, like, about a hundred."

"We'll just say we found this stuff as we've been digging," said Cass. "We can put it together with the rest."

"That's lying," said Hugo.

"It isn't. We're telling the truth about where we found everything. Nobody needs to know exactly when."

"If we hadn't snuck out last night, somebody else might have found these things," I said.

"How could anybody else have known it was there?"

said Cass. "It was Tim's idea. We didn't have a clue until he lifted that rock."

"Somebody was there checking out what we'd been doing—whoever broke the truck window," Tim said.

"Right," she said thoughtfully. "Somebody's been watching us. Remember those footprints?"

A creepy thought. And I had a problem. "What am I going to write down in the Expedition Log about last night? I can't lie in the log. It's an official record."

"You'll figure out something," she said. "Spill something on it so nobody can read it. We've got more important things to think about. This is a once-in-a-lifetime opportunity. We can't blow it. It's so spooky you found that stuff, almost like a sign. An answer to our prayers."

"From the manitous," said Hugo.

"Yeah. Anyway, I'm going up to call *The Beaver*. This has got to work."

Twenty-one

➥

Official Expedition Log
Added to inventory as of July 23

3 two-string white wampum belts
4 three-string purple wampum belts
1 five-string black wampum belt!!
1 false-face mask, carved and painted wood!!
1 false-face mask, wood and straw
4 arrowheads (2 on shafts)
1 quiver (?)
1 carved war club
1 chamois purse with silver (?) coins
8 silver coins
17 loose beads
3 clay pipes
3 beaded bags
1 scalp????

Cass phoned *The Beaver* and talked to a reporter named Alison who said she'd call her back. "She didn't say when, though," Cass said. "It'd better be soon. I hate waiting."

That afternoon when we were swimming, her father bellowed from the top of the hill, "Phone, Cass! It's *The Beaver*."

I ran after Cass, dripping in my towel on the Marlans' deck as she took the call. She listened intently, signaling to me. I got that Alison wanted to come around to do an interview and take pictures. Was tomorrow morning all right?

"You bet." Cass gave her directions to our boathouse. "Woo-hoo!" she cried as she hung up. She flung her arms around me, and we jumped up and down in glee.

For the rest of the day we worked on getting together everything that we'd found—not just the things in the bundle, but all the arrowheads, coins, buttons and broken bits of china we'd dug up, right back to the very first pottery shards from our garden. Tim cut some boards so I could mount things on them with nails and thumbtacks. I was extra careful not to stick the tacks through anything, of course, just around the edges to hold things in place. I wrote labels about where each item was found and when. We decided to leave the bundle in the boathouse until the reporter arrived. That way it would have maximum impact.

We heard the car long before we saw it. It squeaked and groaned up the laneway, an old Lincoln with peeling silver paint. The driver's head barely showed above the wheel. She stepped out and slammed the door.

"Alison Geert from *The Beaver*," she said briskly. "Don't worry about that wreck in your driveway. It always starts." She shrugged a bag of gear onto her shoulder. In black jeans with hair so short it was nearly shaved, she didn't look much older than us. She was only a couple of inches taller than Hugo. "So, let's see this fabulous find of yours."

We all filed into the boathouse. Before showing her our collection, Cass filled her in on the background.

"The place where we've been digging all summer was a big Algonkin trading site way back centuries ago. Hundreds of people lived there, Jesuit priests and everything. It was wiped out by some white people's disease. And the poor guys that survived got attacked by Iroquois. We figure people might have buried their valuables to keep them safe."

168

Alison's eyes glazed a bit. She politely examined my display boards with all the pottery and arrowheads. I could see her wondering how she was going to make a story out of this old stuff. Then Tim reached up into the rafters and lifted down the bundle.

Alison's eyes widened when she saw what was in it. "Now you're talking!" She pulled out her camera. "It's dark in here. Could we move everything outside so I can get some shots?"

"Actually, we were thinking we could go around to the site and take pictures there," Cass said. "It's not that far by car. The road goes all the way now."

"Is that the place they're building that trailer park?" So she knew about it, too.

"Yeah," said Hugo. "With sixty-four electrical outlets."

"Seems to be a hot spot right now." She turned off the little tape recorder clipped to her bag. "Could we sit somewhere for a minute?" She walked out to the end of the dock and kicked off her sandals. "Ahh, that's better," she sighed, paddling her feet in the water.

"You can go for a swim if you want," I said.

"Tempting. I didn't bring a suit, though. I just wanted to go off the record for a minute."

We must have looked puzzled, because she explained. "I mean, I won't report anything you say to me right now. Unless you want me to." We agreed, and she got down to business. "I was pitching this story to my editor when another reporter piped up. He heard on the police short-wave about some vandalism on the same spot."

"At the old Indian village?" Cass said, alarmed.

"Yes. And I don't want to get you guys in trouble, so . . . do you want to tell me anything about that?"

"We've been digging over there," said Tim. "That's not vandalism."

169

"And we had permission," I said.

Before Alison could reply, we heard the sound of another car. Who could it be? A gleaming white vehicle was coming up the lane. With a red light on top. A police cruiser.

Two uniformed officers got out, wearing bulletproof vests and with guns in their holsters—scary. Something about them was familiar, though. "They were at the Bonnycastles' after the break-in," Cass murmured behind me.

"Are your parents around?" the woman officer asked us. "We'd like to speak to them and ask you kids a few questions."

"This is getting interesting," said Alison.

"Remember, you guys swore," Tim muttered as Hugo led the way up the hill. I brought the Expedition Log with me in case it was needed. Alison tagged along at the rear.

Cass went to get her parents, and everybody crowded into our cottage—on the couch, the chairs and the floor. "What's this all about?" Mom asked.

The officers introduced themselves: Constables Sheila Stein and Ted Brais. "We understand these kids have been hanging around the Bonnycastle development across the lake," Constable Stein said.

Cass answered. "We've been searching for artifacts over at the old Algonkin village."

"We saw someone was digging." But that didn't seem to be the problem. "Any of you know anything about a smashed window on a well-drilling rig over there?"

I caught Cass's eye. "I didn't see any well-drilling rig when we were there last time," she said.

"It was moved onto the site on the evening of July 28." Constable Stein checked a notepad. "Sometime during the next twelve hours, somebody put a rock through its windshield."

170

"That's two days ago," said Mom. "Thursday evening. These kids were at home all night. It was my younger son's birthday. And they haven't been off this point since."

Constable Brais wrote it down. "You're sure about that, ma'am?"

"Absolutely. They were over there earlier, but not after dinner."

"What time did they return?"

"I can tell you that. They were supposed to be home by six o'clock. They didn't return until closer to seven."

"What time was the well-drilling machinery moved onto the site?" Cass's dad asked.

"Between eight and nine," said Constable Brais.

"They were home then," Mom said firmly. "At eight o'clock they were in this cottage finishing the dishes and starting a game of Scrabble."

"Which of these kids are yours, Mrs. Greenway?"

Mom pointed to the three of us. "Cass was here as well."

Cass's dad spoke up again. "I had to go to Montreal to pick up my wife." Naomi nodded. "And Cass spent the night here with Rose and the kids. We got back yesterday morning, and none of them have been far out of sight since."

Our parents were giving us an alibi and they didn't even know they were lying! My chest felt tight. I stole a glance at Tim and Hugo. Tim was staring at his knees. Hugo's lips were sealed so hard they were white.

"There was no truck at the site when we left," Cass repeated.

"You didn't notice anything unusual? Anyone hanging around?"

I turned the pages of the Expedition Log. "My brother Hugo found a piece of surveyor's tape on July 18."

171

Constable Brais didn't write it down. "You know that land belongs to Helene Bonnycastle? She says you didn't have permission to dig there."

"The land belongs to Marcel Campbell, who lives near Half Moon Bay," Cass said. "*He* gave us permission."

"He says it belongs to him? That's not my understanding." Officer Brais made a note. "We'll check into it. I know where Campbell lives."

"He's not there now," several of us said at once.

Hugo put up his hand, then stood up, agitated. "I just wanted to say—Mom—"

Oh, no. I crossed my fingers.

"We would never do vandalism," he said solemnly and sat down.

"I'm very glad to hear that," said Constable Stein. She glanced at her partner and they got to their feet. "That should be all for now. Let us know if you think of anything else."

As they left, Alison clicked off her tape recorder. She introduced herself to Mom and Cass's parents. "I'm the summer reporter at *The Beaver*. Hope you didn't mind my being here."

Naomi frowned at her. "I did wonder who you were. I thought you were with the police. I hope you aren't going to try to implicate the kids. As you heard, they had nothing to do with the vandalism."

"I understand that," Alison assured her. "But what I learned will be useful for my story."

"We'll be very interested to see it when it's published," said Jonathan.

"They showed me all the things they've found. They're amazing," Alison said. "Would it be okay if I drove them over to the digging site to get some shots of their discoveries?"

"Tim's grounded," I remembered.

Mom, Naomi and Jonathan briefly conferred. "I think we can make an exception," said Mom. "But no digging."

We all made it into Alison's old Lincoln with room to spare—Cass up front, the rest of us in the back. "It's a heap, isn't it?" Alison patted the dashboard. "My editor sold it to me for $300. He promised me my money back if it doesn't make it through the summer. And he'll buy it back if it does. Seemed like a good deal."

When we came out to the road, the two signs were still firmly in place on the cedar fence. Cass stabbed her finger at the newer one. "Isn't that incredible? You should call that phone number for information. Mrs. Bonnycastle wants to build a trailer park on a sacred native site!"

"Seems crass, all right," Alison agreed.

"I guess we can't knock those signs down now, after what Hugo said about no vandalism," I whispered to Tim. He nodded grimly. He was holding the bundle, now inside a garbage bag to keep it from falling apart.

"Dad says there are least bitterns in there, too," Cass went on to Alison. "They're an endangered species because people have invaded their habitat. Of course, a least bittern wouldn't stop Mrs. Bonnycastle."

"I don't know the woman, but I have a feeling you're right."

"She doesn't need more money. And it's not even her land," Cass said. "It belongs to Marcel."

"Is he the old guy who made a lot of money in the city and came back to Wasamak to retire?"

Cass shook her head. "That doesn't sound like Marcel. He doesn't have any money."

"He doesn't even have electricity," said Hugo.

The new road into the site was as raw as ever, the trees on either side with torn, amputated limbs. Alison rolled

173

down her window and clicked off some shots with her camera. The gravel ended before we got to the well-drilling truck. The Lincoln scraped along until Alison put on the brakes. "This is as far as she goes, folks."

We walked down the road to the drilling rig, staring up at the cab over the mud-spattered grill. Somebody had taped a sheet of plastic over the windshield to keep the rain out. There was broken glass on the ground, like little chips of ice.

Alison took more pictures from several angles. "Okay. Now lead me to the digging site."

Twenty-two

--- ❧ ---

ON TUESDAY MORNING MOM came back from the village with a stack of copies of *The Beaver*. "Come and see this! Alison's story made the front page." She set the stack of papers down. "She's written half the issue. She's done a great job."

We grabbed for copies. I read the headline: "'Major discovery of historical artifacts at native site on Lake Wasamak by young amateur archeologists.' Hey, that's us!"

Underneath were two big pictures. One was a close-up of Tim and Hugo holding the carved masks up to their faces. The other showed us all standing around the rock where we found the treasure, holding shovels and trowels and the broken pick.

"We look like real live archeologists," said Hugo.

"Where on earth did those masks come from?" Mom asked.

"We found them," I said, before Hugo could blurt anything out. We never had got around to telling her about our discovery. "Over at the site—along with a whole lot of other stuff."

At the bottom of the page was a picture of Mrs. Bonnycastle's new sign. "'Local landowner insists on going ahead with plans to build trailer park on sacred site. See page 5,'" Tim read out. "Mrs. Bonnycastle's sure not going to like that."

I turned to page 5. It showed the well-drilling truck with its smashed windshield. That headline read "Vandals or protesters?" Another picture showed the mess made by the new road construction.

I was heading out the door to take a paper to Cass when the phone rang. Mom answered it, then motioned for me to wait. "Yes," she said. "Yes. Oh, yes. No. Of course."

She put down the phone. "How very strange. That was Mr. Bonnycastle. He says those things you found at the site were stolen from his house. He's on his way over. You better get Cass."

Mr. Bonnycastle arrived within fifteen minutes. He was thin with a horsey face and bright blue eyes behind horn-rimmed glasses. His black beard was streaked with gray. He seemed nice, like Cass said, in a professorish sort of way.

He'd brought Roger with him, which was a surprise. Roger looked uncomfortable out of his own territory. He kept sneaking a Game Boy out of his pocket and gazing at it longingly.

Mr. Bonnycastle handed Mom a large envelope. "Some pictures I had taken for insurance purposes." He had an English accent. "You'll see that the false-face masks are an exact match with those in the newspaper photo. I recognized the war club as well." He didn't seem angry, only concerned. "Where are they now?"

Tim had brought the bundle up from the boathouse, and he handed it over. Mr. Bonnycastle opened it and laid out the contents on the floor. Mom looked sort of shocked when she saw what was inside.

Mr. Bonnycastle checked off his list: the masks, arrowheads and spearheads, war club, wampum belts, scalp trophy and chamois bag. "It all seems to be there," he said at last. "We've already replaced many of the things that were taken, but of course these are irreplaceable." He stroked the war club. "This is a very fine piece. See how the shape comes out of the grain of the wood?"

He picked up one of the false faces and turned it over, like he was searching for something. Damage? But then he teased out of the topknot a yellowed bit of paper on a string. "If you need more proof, this one still has the sales tag attached."

I leaned over to read it. "Soth-bys? There's a one and an eight and some zeroes."

"'Suh-the-bees'" Mr. Bonnycastle corrected my pronunciation. "It's an international auction house."

Mom gasped. "Sotheby's! Does that tag actually say $1,800?"

"It was purchased twenty years ago. It would be worth a great deal more today."

"Omigod," said Cass. "We were *playing* with those things! Responsibly, of course," she added.

Yeah, right. Tim chased us around the boathouse with them. "I should have figured there was something fishy," Tim said. "Burlap would have rotted to nothing after all that time." He frowned. "Our fingerprints are on everything. The police won't be able to get clear ones of the burglars'."

"I wouldn't worry," Mr. Bonnycastle assured him. "The thieves likely wore gloves."

"You do believe it wasn't us who stole these things, don't you?" asked Cass. "I mean, there's no way we could have. I was in Montreal and these guys didn't even have a boat they could use. Mrs. Bonnycastle told us the robbers used a boat."

"I didn't for a moment suspect you. Other places on the lake have been burgled over the past year. Ours fits the pattern. What I'm baffled by is how these things got over to that piece of land and under a rock. Someone hid them, obviously—but who? It's far too peculiar to be coincidental." He looked around at us more sternly. "Are you sure you don't know anything about it?"

We shook our heads. But then Tim spoke up. "I remember when I started digging around the rock thinking that the earth was loose. But I figured it was because of a groundhog or something."

"And what exactly was it you were all searching for so intently?"

"Native artifacts." I pointed to the display boards on the mantel. "Those are things we found ourselves; I mean, besides your things."

Mr. Bonnycastle got up to look. "You found all these at the site?"

"Most of them. The labels tell where everything comes from."

He read them carefully, even borrowing a pencil to make some changes. "This is French bead, not wampum. That is, it was brought from Europe as trade goods. And this arrowhead is Iroquois, not Algonkin. But you've done a fine job," he told me.

"So that's proof that native people were on that site," Cass reminded him. "Like you always said. It's not so spectacular as what's in the bundle, but it still shows the land is incredibly historic. That's what we wanted to prove. Now it has to be preserved as a heritage site. Mrs. Bonnycastle can't build a trailer park on it."

Mr. Bonnycastle frowned. "I agree it isn't the right thing to do. I haven't been able to convince my wife of that, unfortunately. Having it designated as a significant site wouldn't be an easy process. These things take time and political will. There haven't been more than a handful of Algonkins in this area for centuries. Local people say there's a native burial ground there, but that's just hearsay. Any bones would have long since disappeared. In fact, some archeology students from McGill University asked permission to dig last year, but I don't believe anything ever came of it."

"Our friend Marcel Campbell says the land belongs to him," I said, "not Mrs. Bonnycastle."

Mr. Bonnycastle nodded. "I know Marcel. I expect he's speaking in terms of an Algonkin land claim. He's right, in that the land was taken from the Algonkins by mistake. The British believed it belonged to the Mississauga, and that's whom they bought it from. But that happened well over two hundred years ago. It's too late now to turn back the clock."

He began packing the contents of the bundle in a box he'd brought. We watched glumly. Cass burst out, "Can't you at least stall Mrs. Bonnycastle until Marcel comes back? He's gone away, so we haven't even been able to tell him what's happening."

Mr. Bonnycastle cleared his throat. "It's my wife's decision. She's determined to go ahead. I can't order her not to." He looked around for Roger, who was lurking in the doorway, his Game Boy making electronic peepings. "Put that infernal thing away and give me a hand."

"But what if it's not her land?" I asked.

"She's having a survey done, to be absolutely in the clear. I've done a little research myself from a historical point of view. There's some confusion over the boundaries, because the original creek bed appears to have been disturbed by a beaver dam. Of course, Helene won't proceed until that's straightened out."

"But she *is* proceeding!" Cass cried. "She's put up a sign advertising the trailer park already!"

He looked surprised. "I wasn't aware of that. Well, ah,

179

you see, if there is a boundary problem, I don't believe it will make much difference. She'll just move the project a hundred yards or so to where she has undisputed title. Of course, that would mean filling in swamp."

"That would be destroying wetlands. She won't be allowed to do it. There's least bitterns living there. They're very rare."

"Endangered," I said.

Mr. Bonnycastle seemed more embarrassed than ever. "I believe they *will* let her do it. Helene usually gets her way with the local council." He saw our dismayed faces. "It was bound to happen sooner or later," he said kindly. "A hundred years ago there was a push to make this into a resort area. It's taken a long time, but the town wants it. No one makes much of a living from farming."

Cass's face was bleak. "It will ruin the lake!"

"Surely others have a right to enjoy it as you do?"

"They don't look after it!" She clenched her fists. "There was a nest of loons near us for my whole life, and it's been washed out by stupid people with big boats. And now there'll be more and more of them!" She burst into angry tears. "It's okay for you, way over on the other side of the lake. If Mrs. Bonnycastle wants a trailer park, why doesn't she build it over by your place?"

He cleared his throat. "I admit, she doesn't want it in our backyard."

"Well, it's in ours! Oh, I'm not going to cry," she wailed and rushed out of the cottage. The screen door banged behind her.

Mom broke the silence that followed. "It's an upsetting situation for her. For all of us."

Mr. Bonnycastle stood up. "What an old hypocrite I've become. Terrible to think that unspoiled nature is a luxury. And we stand by and witness the loss. To be honest,

180

it's a touchy subject in our family. It's quite a preoccupation with my wife's nephew."

"Who, Paul?" That was weird.

"Surely he's talked to you?"

"About what?" I asked.

"This trailer park. He's been fighting about it with Helene since he arrived. And now she's found out he's been writing letters to try to stop it."

"Why is he doing that?" Tim asked.

"Well, exactly. Why? Helene feels it's none of his business."

While Mom walked Mr. Bonnycastle to his car, I tried to digest all the new information. My head was spinning.

"Should we go see if Cass is okay?" Hugo asked.

"She'll be fine. I bet it was him over at the site the other night," Tim said to himself.

"Who—Mr. Bonnycastle?" I asked.

"No, Paul."

"He goes out at night all the time," said a voice from the doorway.

I looked up in surprise. Roger was still there, on the other side of the screen.

"At night?" Tim asked.

"I hear him."

Tim thought for a moment. "What about Thursday night?"

"Can't remember." Roger fidgeted with the door catch. "I came back to ask something. I did a search for 'Algonkin' on the Internet. I got 7,100 hits."

We stared at him. What on earth was he talking about?

"I've got to narrow it down," he went on. "I put in 'Lake Wasamak,' but nothing showed up. Can you think of any other key words?"

181

"I don't know what you're searching for," I said, totally mystified.

"Algonkins. To help you find out about them."

I sighed. "Never mind. It doesn't matter anymore."

But Roger just waited. I tried to think of something to tell him so he'd go away. "Fur trade? Jesuit priests?"

After a moment he nodded, then left.

"That's one spooky kid," said Tim. "Interesting what he said about Paul, though."

Could it have been Paul we glimpsed that night at Half Moon Bay, the dark shadow shooting across the water? Maybe it was him that I saw way back at the start of the summer, too. "Why don't we talk to him?"

"There's definitely a few things I'd like to ask him," Tim said.

Twenty-three

❧

Hugo and I found Cass on her dock, staring out at the water. She turned when she heard our footsteps. "What took you so long? I can't see there was anything left to say." Her face was pale and streaky.

"Not about the trailer park," I said. "But we did find out something about Paul."

"You're the one who's interested in Paul, not me."

"That's not fair, Cass." I felt my face blaze. "Mr. Bonnycastle said Paul's upset about the trailer park, like we are. Tim thinks Paul was over at the site. Maybe it was Paul who broke the truck window." I had her attention now. "Mr. Bonnycastle thought we were friends with Paul because he feels the same way we do about the trailer park. So would you phone Paul and say we want to talk to him?"

"Why don't you do it?"

"You'd be better at it than me."

"It's not going to make any difference."

"He might be able to tell us something."

"Then phone loverboy yourself," she sneered.

I stared at Cass in disbelief, but she wouldn't look at me. "Why are you being so horrible?" I stomped away with Hugo behind me. I'd never say anything like that to a friend.

But I didn't like being out of sorts with Cass. After lunch I figured she'd be back to her old self, so I tried again. She was stretched out on the lounger on her deck, eating plums and spitting the pits over the railing. She didn't even look up when Hugo and I climbed the steps. A bad sign.

I took a deep breath. "Cass, we feel just as bad about the trailer park as you do. But it doesn't do any good to get so upset."

She sat up, glaring. "It makes me really angry to hear you say that, Leia. If you're not upset, then you're giving up. You're a quitter."

I blinked. "Who said anything about giving up?"

"We *can't* give up," she said fiercely. "And if you do, you're a rotten traitor and I'll never speak to you again. I'm thinking of going on a hunger strike. Maybe I'll chain myself to the Bonnycastles' front door and get Alison to do another story. 'Girl Starves to Death to Save Wilderness.'"

"You'd have to stop eating, then," her father called from inside the cottage.

"I could if I wanted," she shouted back. "And Dad, what are you doing? You're always going on about that stupid least bittern, but you're not doing anything constructive to save it. You're just sitting on your behind."

He came to the doorway. "Hey, low blow. I'm busy working on my book."

"You're a spineless sellout like the rest of them."

"Pardon me?" he roared. "Spineless?"

I fled, still stinging from Cass calling me a quitter. Saying I was giving up, when I wasn't at all. Besides, what did she know about giving up? There were lot of things I'd had to give up—my house, my school, my dad. Adults make decisions for you, and there isn't much you can do. You live with it. How could she talk to me that way anyway, her eyes all cold and angry like she didn't even know me?

When we were doing the supper dishes, Tim asked what was wrong. I'd washed my face, but I guess he could see I'd been crying.

184

"Nothing." Only the big lump sitting in my stomach. "Cass is being horrible."

"Yeah. And?"

"I don't see why she has to take it out on me. I feel the same way she does."

"She likes to push people around. And you let her do it to you."

"I don't!"

"Yes, you do. You do whatever she wants."

"But I *like* her," I wailed. "She's great. She's interesting, and I'm not."

Tim stopped wiping the plate in his hand and stared at me.

"Well, it's true, Tim! I'm ordinary!" He didn't deny it.

He began wiping the plate again, then put it away and took a new one. "You're better than her."

I blinked back more tears. He had to say that. He was my brother. But I didn't want to be better than Cass. I just didn't want to lose her as my friend.

Next day after lunch Cass breezed in the screen door like nothing had happened. "'Lo, dudes. What's everybody up to?"

We were just taking it easy, for a change. Hugo was making a frog house out of an ice-cream tub and screening. Tim was doing something with his fishing rod. I was reading.

"Nothing much," said Tim. "How's the hunger strike going?"

Cass helped herself to an apple from the bowl and threw herself down on the couch beside me. "I'm bored, okay? It's a sunny day—isn't anybody going digging?"

"Too hot," said Hugo.

"We're giving up," I said sarcastically, without looking up from my book.

Nobody else said anything. "Anybody want to play Monopoly?" Cass asked hopefully.

"No!" said Tim.

"Aww," said Hugo, disappointed. "I do."

She tried another approach. "Did you guys phone Paul yet?"

I lowered my book. It wasn't that exciting. "He probably wouldn't talk to us anyway."

"Why not? He owes us an explanation." She jumped up to get the phone book and looked up the Bonnycastles' number. "Okay?" When nobody said anything, she shrugged. "Well, here goes."

She dialed, listened for a moment and then asked for Paul. "Carmen answered," she hissed, hand over the receiver. "You'd think she never heard of the guy. She doesn't know where he is, but she's gone to see if she can find him." Minutes passed. "At least I think she did."

Her face changed. Somebody had answered. "Hi, Paul," she said brightly. "It's Cass Marlan. We met over at your aunt's place a couple of times. Your uncle thinks we should talk." She paused. "Well, I guess he thought we *were* talking." She rushed on. "How about meeting us over at the old Indian village at Half Moon Bay? You know where I mean—where your *aunt* wants to build the *trailer park*."

He must have agreed, because she started giving directions. "You can't miss it. We've made a channel in through the rushes. Right now, actually. Meet you in half an hour." Another pause while she listened. "Okay, well, as soon as you can."

"I don't know why you told him how to get there," said Tim. "He found it on his own okay the other night."

We were at the site in twenty minutes. Paul wasn't there yet, and since we hadn't brought digging tools, there was nothing to do but wait. Tim walked out to the road, then called back, "The well-drilling truck's gone."

"They probably took it away to fix the windshield," said Cass. "It'll be back. Nothing's changed."

Hugo was turning over rocks. He straightened and yelled, "Guys, see what I found!" He held out his hand. I was expecting to see an arrowhead or a coin or pottery shards, but it was a salamander, small enough to fit in his palm. The body was black, the legs and tail speckled with blue, like it had been splashed with paint. "Neat, eh? Like it's made out of rubber."

"Cool," said Tim, but his heart wasn't in it.

"Be sure to put it back exactly where you found it," I said.

"'Course I will." Hugo sounded disappointed by our lack of enthusiasm. "I'm being gentle with it."

I kept watch for Paul. Cass had told him to be there in half an hour, and nearly an hour had gone by. Maybe he was having trouble paddling. The wind was raising white-caps out on the lake. I spotted a dark speck in the distance, but it turned out to be somebody fishing. Maybe Paul wasn't coming after all. Maybe he'd just said he would to get Cass off the phone.

The hour passed. Then I saw another speck. It grew larger. A boat, with one person in it, at the back. I pointed. "Is that him?"

Cass squinted. "Man, have you got good eyes."

When the boat turned into the channel in the reeds, I could see it was a dark green canoe. Paul stepped out onto a grassy clump and pulled his boat up. He looked self-conscious walking toward us, his head down. But then he straightened and flicked his hair out of his eyes.

"Sorry I'm late. I got held up, and there was a head-wind." Something about him was different. He'd cut his

187

hair so the bleached ends were mostly gone. It was also the first time I'd seen him without his headset. "What did you want to talk about?"

"I think you know," said Cass.

He shoved his hands deep into his pockets. "You mean the stuff I planted and you found?"

We stared at him. "You planted it?" said Tim.

"Isn't that why you got me over here? I thought you had it figured out."

Tim was the one who broke the shocked silence. "Why were you trying to get us in trouble? We never did anything to you."

"I wasn't trying to get you in trouble."

"Sure seems like it."

"The police came around asking us all kinds of questions," said Cass angrily. "They thought we broke the truck window. Lucky we had alibis." Then she thought of something else. "Now that they know where the stuff came from, they'll think we stole it to make it seem like a big discovery."

Paul said nothing, just dug a hole in the sand with his shoe.

"So you stole it from your aunt and uncle and buried it here?" Cass asked.

His head shot up. "I didn't steal it. I found it."

"Oh, yeah, like on the library walls?" Tim said.

"No, down near the water in the bushes. The B-and-E guys dropped them."

"You saw them?"

"I didn't know anything about it until the police came. First I heard about it was when Carmen and Manuel woke me up and said the police wanted to talk to me."

"Then how did you get the things?" Tim asked.

"I told you—I found them. They must have been in a

hurry to get to their boat. All the native stuff was in the one bag, and they must have dropped it going down the hill. I went out early the next morning and found it."

Tim looked like he didn't believe him. "How come you found it and not the police?"

"It was dark. Pouring rain."

"Why didn't you tell your aunt?"

He made a face. "The cops grilled me, like I was in on it. An inside job. I figured if I turned up with the stuff— 'Just found it in the bushes,' yeah, right—Aunt Helene would think I was mixed up in the robbery after all. And that would have given her a perfect excuse to send me away. So I hid the artifacts in the boathouse until I could think of something."

"Then how did the bundle get over here?" Cass asked.

"I saw you digging the place up, and that gave me the idea. I found some old burlap in the compost heap to wrap the stuff in and hid it all under a rock—but not very well, so you'd find it. Took you long enough."

"You *wanted* us to find it?"

"Yeah. I was hoping when you did, everybody'd think there was more buried here, and that'd stop Aunt Helene from building. For a while, anyway."

"That's what we tried to do, too," I said. "We got a story in the paper."

"I saw it."

"But sooner or later people were bound to figure out that those things came from your aunt and uncle's place," said Tim.

"I didn't say it was a great plan. And since that story came out in *The Beaver*, some magazine reporter called up to interview my aunt. She blew. She told the reporter it's just a plot a bunch of kids cooked up."

189

We stared at him in horror. "So we've all made it worse instead of better," Cass said.

"Yup."

Nobody could think of anything to say. Except Tim. "Okay, I get all that, but why did you break the truck windshield? You knew we were hanging around. Still seems to me you were trying to frame us."

Paul started scuffing the ground again. "That was stupid, breaking that window. But I didn't do it to get you in trouble."

"Admit it—you didn't care if you got us in trouble or not!" Tim clenched his fists.

"I do dumb things, okay?" said Paul, raising his voice. "I get mad and I do something stupid. That's my problem. So turn me into the police, I don't care. It's not going to make any difference to Aunt Helene."

"What I can't figure out is why this is all such a big deal for you," Tim persisted. "You can go back to your fancy school and never stay with your aunt again. So why do you care what happens in some old swamp?"

"Haven't you figured that out either?" he sneered. "I thought you guys were smart."

I knew. "You're Algonkin, aren't you?"

He looked at me. "Bingo."

Twenty-four

—— ➤ ——

THE CROWS WOKE ME WITH THEIR CROAKING and wheedling. I pulled the covers over my ears and tried to go back to sleep, but it was too late. My brain was already awake. Yesterday came flooding back.

Paul was Algonkin—that part was amazing. Algonkin, like the people who lived in Half Moon Bay, the people we'd been looking for all summer. Maybe they were even his ancestors. No wonder he didn't like the idea of the trailer park.

Then I remembered why I had butterflies in my stomach. We'd come home from Half Moon Bay to hear that a reporter from *Maclean's* wanted to talk to us. What were we going to say? We agreed nobody would breathe a word about how the bundle got under the rock. But Paul said that Mrs. Bonnycastle had already told a reporter it was a plot. Did she know that Paul was responsible? It would be hideously embarrassing if it all came out. Mrs. Bonnycastle would get her way for sure.

I put on my clothes, peering at myself in the mirror. My bangs were in my eyes. I picked up the nail scissors and trimmed them back above my eyebrows. It left a white line where the sun hadn't reached my skin. I looked like a ten-year-old.

No one else was awake. I went down to the dock and lay on the sun-warmed wood, watching the fish going about their business. It made me feel better. They didn't seem to be worried about anything in their silent green world.

191

Something made me lift my head—a noise, maybe. On the far side of the rocks where Cass and I usually snorkeled, a loon was floating on the surface of the lake. So close up, dramatic black and white, it looked huge— the size of a dachshund. Could it be the father or mother from the nest? Cass kept insisting we should have seen the chicks by now. She was certain that the speedboats had washed out the nest. But just because we hadn't seen any chicks didn't mean they weren't there.

The loon got within five feet of me before it opened its beak and made a weird noise, a crazy little laugh—ha-ha-ha. Then it dove. Farther out, another one surfaced. Two smaller heads popped up beside it. Little loons! The chicks!

I had to tell Cass! She'd be so thrilled she probably wouldn't even mind being woken up to be told. I got to my feet carefully, so I wouldn't frighten the loons. Out beyond them, a boat appeared around the point—a dark green canoe. It had to be Paul.

He was coming straight toward me. The idea of talking to him on my own made me excited and scared at the same time. If only I hadn't cut my stupid bangs! Maybe he'd just wave from a distance and go on by.

Instead, he came right into the dock. He had a red bandanna tied around his head, and he was wearing sunglasses, so I couldn't see his eyes. Still, he was a lot more cheerful than I expected after yesterday. He took his headset off. "Guess what?" He was actually sort of smiling. "Marcel's back."

Marcel! Fantastic! Finally, we'd sort out this mess.

"I was out for a paddle last night and saw his light. I'm heading over there now. You want to come?"

"Will he be awake this early?"

"He gets up at six. And he's got a fire on." Paul pointed

across the bay at a near-invisible wisp of smoke rising into the clear morning air.

"Everybody's still asleep," I said reluctantly. "We'll have to go over later."

"You're up. Want to come now?"

"Just me?" I said stupidly.

He nodded.

"They'd kill me if I went to see Marcel and didn't tell them."

"Leave a note."

I tore up the hill. I was scribbling something on the back of an envelope when I heard Tim cough. I stuck my head in his room and whispered his name. He lifted his head groggily.

"Marcel's come back. I'm going over with Paul to see him. Tell Mom and Hugo and Cass, okay?"

Both his eyes were open now, but I didn't wait for an answer. Rushing back down the hill, I got a paddle and life jacket from the boathouse. Paul was still waiting.

"Sorry I took so long," I said, trying to catch my breath.

"You were hardly any time at all." Paul steadied the canoe while I lowered myself on the seat in the bow. At least he'd be looking at the back of my head, not at my butchered bangs.

The bottom of his canoe gleamed. In Cass's you always had to climb over muddy tools and sandals and Mars bar wrappers. "This is a really beautiful boat."

"It's Aunt Helene's. I'm the only one who uses it, though."

"I never paddled before this summer. Tell me if I'm doing it wrong."

"You're doing okay."

We were the only ones on the lake except for a couple of fishermen. It was so quiet that our paddles dipping in

193

the water sounded loud. I matched my paddling to his. "I think I saw you in our bay once," I said. "In the evening. Really early in the summer."

"Could have been." He wasn't giving anything away.

"How come you go out in the canoe so much?" It sounded dumb as soon as I said it, but he answered.

"I used to paddle around a lot with my dad when I was little. Once we saw a moose and calf. Besides, there's nothing else to do. Those enough reasons?"

"Yes," I said hastily. "Is it your dad who's Algonkin or your mom?"

"My dad."

I asked him how he was related to Mrs. Bonnycastle. I couldn't figure that part out.

"She and my mom are sisters."

He filled in the basic story. "It kinda goes back before I was born, to my dad and mom getting together."

"Did they meet around here?"

"No, in Ottawa, at college. They started going out. And my mom's father—he was Aunt Helene's dad, too—he wasn't that happy about it. He liked collecting native stuff, but I guess he wasn't so keen about having a live one in his family."

After his parents got married and he was born, Paul said, they used to come to the lake every summer. "I can't remember my grandfather very well—I was really young when he died and he was pretty old. He mostly spoke French and my family mostly talked English. I can't remember, you know, ever sitting on his lap or anything.

"Then he died and Aunt Helen got the cottage and some other land around the lake. My mom didn't get hardly anything in the will. My dad figured it was because she married him. Anyway, after that he and Aunt Helene didn't get along so well. Especially when he joined a group working to reclaim traditional lands. My aunt says it's nonsense. She says there were no Indians around here when she was growing up."

"What about Marcel?"

"She calls him an old phoney. She hates him calling his property Algonkin land."

"But it is."

"Yeah. Anyway, you can understand why my folks didn't come here after that. Then they moved to California."

"California! That's neat. Didn't you want to go?"

"I did go. Their house is okay, but so you can grow lemons in your backyard? Big deal. There's nothing to do unless you have a car, and it's not like I can get a job. So I've been going to school in Canada. Last summer I stayed in Toronto with my friend, but his family moved out West. Aunt Helene let me come here this year. We started fighting right away, and when I found out about her big trailer-park plan, it got worse."

We paddled in silence for a minute. "What about you?" he said. "What's your story?"

"Not so interesting." I told him some stuff about living in Port Hope and then moving to Toronto. He knew right where we lived.

"Toronto's okay," he said. "I take the bus downtown from school sometimes on the weekend. Go and buy music or just walk around. It's cool."

We were almost across the bay now. "I told Aunt Helene I broke the window of that well-drilling truck," he said.

I turned around. "Did you get in a lot of trouble?"

"Yeah...but no more than I was in already. A lot of screaming and yelling. I said I was sorry and that it was a stupid thing to do. I said I'd pay for it. I was freaking out that she was going to send me away. She still might."

"Did you tell her about—you know—hiding those things under the rock?"

"Not yet."

"Maybe you don't have to."

"If I don't, she'll figure it out."

We were almost at the shore. I got ready to jump out. I didn't want him to think he had to help me—take my hand or anything. But he just held the boat steady for me with his paddle. And when he got out, I noticed he was wearing moccasins.

Marcel wasn't in his cabin, but it smelled like coffee, so he had to be around. I figured he might be in his garden. When we went up the hill, the door to his stockade was open. I heard whistling. Marcel was tying up his tomato plants.

He straightened slowly when he saw Paul and me and gave us a wave and a huge grin. "Who I got to thank for keeping my garden watered?"

"Us," I said.

"Me," said Paul at the same time.

I burst out laughing. I'd been going to apologize to Marcel for not watering enough. Now it turned out Paul had been watering, too.

"That's why she grow so good." Marcel gazed past us. "Only two of you? Where de rest?"

"Still asleep," said Paul. "Where have you been all this time?"

"In de city."

It was hard to picture Marcel with his bent back and shabby clothes on busy streets crowded with high buildings. "We were worried something happened to you."

"Personal business." He said it like *bidness*. "Too much talking, talking. I t'ink you been busy, too?"

There was so much to tell him. "It's Mrs. Bonnycastle who's building the trailer park on your land in Half Moon Bay," I blurted out. "She says it's her land, but it's yours."

"I 'ear about that." He wiped his hands on his trousers. "So maybe we 'ave some breakfast, eh?"

Was that all he was going to say? Paul and I exchanged a glance. He shrugged. Marcel hooked the gate behind us and led the way slowly down the hill. I waited for him to tell us not to worry, to say that he'd stop Mrs. Bonnycastle and her plans and everything would be all right. But he just puttered around his woodstove making toast and heating up the coffee.

Paul wasn't saying anything either. I started telling Marcel about how we'd been digging for evidence to prove the site was historic. "Mrs. Bonnycastle doesn't care about that, though. And she says it's her land."

Marcel handed us each a mug. "I been checking into dat. Maybe you see some surveyors round de old camp?"

Paul blew on his coffee. "About two weeks ago?"

I remembered the length of orange tape Hugo had found.

Marcel nodded. "I hire dem. I know I own to de river, my deed say so. An' I know Pierre Mercier—" he glanced at Paul, "your gran'fadder—he own de other side. So de old village, dat is on my side of de river, eh? But I find out dat some long time ago—twenty, thirty year—de river, she move. Beaver dam up one way, river find another way."

"You mean the river once used to be on this side of the village?" Paul asked.

"Dat is true. So part of de land I t'ink I buy ten year ago don't really belong to me. Already belong Pierre Mercier,

197

then his daughter Helene. Her deed goes back long way. Mine is wort'less bit of paper—all I got is thirty meter of swamp."

The bad news sank in. "Geez." Paul's face closed, his mouth a thin line. "I was so sure when you came back, it would be okay. I should have known. That's not how it works. Nothing's ever easy," he said bitterly.

I heard voices outside, and someone hammered at the door. Marcel went to open it. Hugo was standing there, Tim and Cass behind him.

Hugo pulled a license plate and a plastic lighter from his pack. He held them out to Marcel. "I've been collecting stuff for your totem. I found them on the road." He watched Marcel's face. "Are they good ones?"

Marcel took them with a smile. "Now dat is kind of you. I know right where these go. Come in, come in."

The room filled up and everybody started talking at once. "I t'ink you all got bigger," Marcel said, laughing. "Sit down, sit down." He refilled the coffeepot. "You been very busy, I 'ear. I t'ink you prove that village was there for sure."

"Where've you been anyway?" Cass asked. "Did you hear about Mrs. Bonnycastle's trailer park? You're the only one who can stop it."

"Except it's not his land," said Paul.

"*What?*" Cass practically shouted.

"Marcel says the campsite is actually on Mrs. Bonnycastle's land," I said.

While Marcel calmly spread our toast with raspberry jam, he told the story all over again.

"Now it makes sense," Tim said.

"I'm glad you think so," Cass snorted. If the room had been bigger, she would have paced. "I can't believe it. One more disaster." She filled Marcel in about our discovery that turned out to be stolen. "That really backfired," she said, glaring at Paul. "So now his aunt claims we're in this big conspiracy to make it seem like the land is important when it isn't."

"We found other things that prove it is," I said. "But Mr. Bonnycastle says his wife doesn't care."

Marcel looked around at our long faces. "Maybe not so bad as you t'ink."

"What could possibly be good about it?" Cass said angrily. "Don't tell us there's a bright side, because there isn't. Everything's all screwed up."

Marcel passed the toast. "In Montreal I find out some'ting you might like to know."

"What were you doing in Montreal?" I asked. I took some toast and waited for him to sit down and start talking again. Finally he settled in his chair.

"Las' summer, some students were digging round 'ere. You know about dat? I never learn what dey find. Could be important, I t'ink. So I go to university to find out. Only, all offices empty, professors an' students *en vacance*. At las' I find some person who turn on the computer an' print somet'ing for me." He pointed to a large envelope on the table. "Look at that."

Paul reached for it at the same time as Tim. This time they didn't fight. Tim took out some papers stapled together like a school project. "Results of Dig at Lake Wasamak, Site of 17th- and 18th-Century Algonkin Settlement," he read.

We crowded around. Some pages had pictures. Most were of our digging site—I recognized the birch trees out near the road. One showed a huge rock the size of a car.

"Hey, I know that rock," Hugo said.

"Keep reading," Marcel prompted.

Tim ran his finger down a paragraph highlighted in

199

yellow. "This is...uh about an epidemic that killed a whole bunch of people."

"Like you told us, Marcel," I remembered. "All the people in the village got sick and died."

"So many people die, no place an' nobody lef' to bury dem."

"It says that here," Tim said. "There's a letter from some Jesuit priest writing back to France." He read it out. *"They piled the dead in a natural hollow in the land and covered them with a thin scraping of frozen earth. All those who were yet strong enough to stand gathered together and rolled a great stone over the place to keep it from being disturbed by wild beasts."*

He raised his head. "Do you think 'great stone' means that huge rock on the site?"

"It's way too big to move," I said.

Tim thought about it. "Twenty people could do it, maybe."

"Is that what those archeology students were searching for?" said Cass. "Dead bodies?"

He read farther down. "I don't think they actually did any digging. They're *going* to, if they get money to do it, and permission."

"Permission from Mrs. Bonnycastle? I don't think so," said Cass.

"Permission from the band whose ancestors are buried there, it should be," said Paul.

Cass got to her feet. "Well, we're not going to ask anybody's permission. We don't have time. We have to get digging."

Paul shook his head. "You can't disturb the dead."

"We won't be disturbing them. We only need to *find* them. Not even your aunt can build a trailer park on top of dead people." She turned to Marcel. "Right, Marcel? What do you think?"

For a long while, he just stared ahead, lost in his thoughts. "I agree with Paul," he said finally. "Not a good t'ing, disturbing de dead. But..." He paused again. "If it come to saving de land, maybe de dead should 'ave their say."

Twenty-five

———— ❧ ————

I COULD SEE THE BIG ROCK EVEN from the channel. We'd been looking at it all summer. We'd even climbed on it. The only way I made it to the top was with Tim giving me a leg up.

Now we walked slowly around it. "I forgot how big that puppy is," Cass said. "We'll never move it. Not without a front-end loader."

"We don't have to." Tim slapped at a horsefly. "Not if hundreds of people died, like that priest said. Even a rock this big wouldn't cover that many bodies. Some of them must be right under our feet. See how the ground's sunk down lower there?"

I took several steps back, goosebumps on my arms.

"We should try digging right here," Tim said. "I bet we'll find something."

"Skeletons," said Hugo in a hollow voice. We weren't hunting for arrowheads anymore.

My shovel hit a sumac root right away. The sandy soil was so choked with them it was tough to make headway. Tim whacked at the bushes with an ax.

Paul just stood and watched. He didn't dig. Of course, he was wearing moccasins, so he couldn't really. But Cass didn't notice that. She kept glowering at him. "You could help us, you know. The exercise wouldn't hurt you."

"I got this idea that kids aren't supposed to dig up aboriginal burial grounds. Just a hunch there's some kind of law about that," Paul replied.

"Well, your plan didn't work out that great, did it?"

He glared and moved a little ways off, but he didn't leave. None of us had a watch, but I could tell from how far the sun had moved that we'd been digging for quite a while. And we were getting absolutely nowhere. Hugo quit and went to hunt salamanders. Tim was digging ten feet away from where we had first started. "Why are you way over there?" Cass asked irritably. "We should all be digging in the same place. Otherwise it'll take forever to go deep enough."

Tim ignored her. He was doing what he always did—he had an idea in his head and he was going at it. But this time I could see it was really bugging Cass. She flung down her shovel and stormed off.

When she didn't come back in a few minutes, I went after her. She was sitting on a log throwing snail shells into the channel. "Are you okay?"

"Of course I'm okay. I'm just sick of digging. We haven't done anything else all summer."

That was ironic, coming from her. Whose idea was all of this in the first place? And now she was complaining? But I didn't say that. Then another thought crossed my mind.

"Is the idea of bodies getting to you?"

"No!" She glared. "It's your brother—Tim. He always has to do everything his way." She flung more shells. "And Paul just stands around doing nothing. I don't think there's anything there anyway."

"But the priest's letter said—"

She snorted. "That was three hundred years ago. Just because it's old doesn't mean it's true. The letter might not even be talking about the same place. Probably the river moved again and it's the wrong rock. And we'll just keep on digging and digging for no reason." Her voice rose. "And then it'll be too late. But you won't care about that."

203

"What do you mean, Cass? Of course I care!"

"I mean you'll be at your dad's and I'll be here by myself, watching this place get made into a trailer park!"

"We won't be leaving for another ten days, Cass. Lots can change in that time. And Paul will still be here."

"What use is he? I wish he'd just go away and stop causing trouble. We were doing fine until he came along and wrecked things."

"He didn't mean to."

"You so sure about that? But you always have to give everybody the benefit of the doubt, don't you?"

My heart sank. "You're mad at me for going to Marcel's with Paul, aren't you? I knew you would be. But I told Tim to wake you up."

"Oh, shut up, Miss Goody Two-shoes! I don't care where you go or who you go with." Then she muttered, "You could have waited."

My eyes stung with tears. I couldn't stand her glaring at me in that mean way.

"Quit picking on my sister." Tim was standing on the rise behind us. "What's she ever done, except exactly what you want?"

Cass stood up and strode toward him. I thought she was going to punch him. "What *I* want?" she cried, waving her arms, nearly nose to nose with him. "You're the one who always has to be the big man in control!"

Hugo appeared, eyes wide with dismay. And Paul was there, too, watching us all fighting and yelling. Everything was going wrong. The summer was unraveling in front of my eyes.

"I wasn't trying to wreck everything," Paul said. He must have heard what Cass said about him.

She turned on him. "Don't flatter yourself! Your aunt's doing a fine job without any help from you."

He took a deep breath. "I know how you feel."

"You know how I *feel*?" Her words dripped sarcasm. "Tell me then."

"Helpless." His voice was low but steady. "Things go wrong and you can't fix them, no matter how hard you try. So you get pissed off at everybody."

"You should talk—the guy who throws rocks through windshields!"

He ducked his head. "I know. I messed up—again. But maybe you're smarter than me. You're luckier, anyway. You've got parents and friends to help you."

Cass hooted. "Oh, yeah! I've got such *great* parents. What are they doing to help? Nothing! A big fat zero. My dad says he has to work on his *important* book, and my mother spends all her time at her job. So what if I'm lucky? What difference does that make?" She waved her arms around some more. "And you're giving me advice? You sound like a social worker—probably because you have one. Anyway, I *am* doing something. I'm digging, aren't I? You're not."

Paul scuffed the ground. "I was thinking I'd go over to Marcel's and borrow an ax from him."

"Yeah? To cut your head off?" Then she threw a whole handful of snail shells into the swamp. "Okay, okay, I get it. I'm being a jerk again." Her eyes reddened. "I'm just *so* frustrated. I was so sure as soon as Marcel came back everything would be fixed."

"That's what we all thought," I said.

We dragged ourselves back to the hole and our shovels, and Paul took off in the canoe for Marcel's. He was gone so long Cass started grumbling about him all over again. But finally the canoe came around the point. It had two people in it now—Paul and a short, shaggy figure in the bow.

"Hey, Marcel!" Hugo crowed.

205

I was incredibly glad to see him—an adult, but not like an adult. "I brought youse rations," he called out to us, holding up a plastic bread bag full of sandwiches. Suddenly I realized I was starving. I hadn't eaten anything since that toast he made us and that seemed like days ago. Paul followed, carrying an ax and a big jug of water.

Marcel set the food down on a flat-topped boulder and everybody grabbed. I sank my teeth into soft white bread and bologna dripping with mayonnaise. I'd never tasted anything so good.

Paul gulped down a sandwich and went over to the hole with the ax. I noticed he'd changed his shoes. He set to work on the matted roots, and by the time I picked up a shovel again, he'd cleared a big area.

The earth came out a lot more easily now. We removed it carefully and Marcel and Hugo sorted through the growing pile of roots and dirt and stones. They found some shells and shards of pottery.

Nobody talked much. Cass wiped her sweaty face, smearing it with grime. "Shouldn't we have found something by now?"

Tim caught my eye: *Here we go again.* But I was feeling discouraged, too. Maybe it wasn't the right spot after all. Or maybe Tim was wrong and all the bones *were* underneath the rock where we couldn't get at them.

A few minutes later, Tim called out, "Hey, I think—"

We put down our shovels and gathered around as he scraped the earth away from what he'd found. It was long like a stick and yellowish-brown. Marcel leaned over it. "Bone, for sure."

Cass and I got trowels and climbed back in the hole. We cleared the dirt away from a smaller bone beside the long one, and then another. And more bones. Maybe a leg and part of a foot.

A person's leg. Somebody's foot.

Paul straightened up. "Can we stop now?"

We parted ways with Paul and Marcel at the point and headed across the bay for home. As we were tying up the boat, Mom and Cass's mother appeared at the top of the path.

"Are we going to tell Mom about the bones?" Hugo whispered.

"Wait," I whispered back. "They look like they're upset."

"There's been a summons from Mrs. Bonnycastle," Naomi said. "She wants you all over there ASAP. Command performance. The nerve of that woman. No way you kids are going into this on your own."

"Get cleaned up and we'll drive you over," said Mom.

"But Mom, I'm exhausted," wailed Hugo.

They took in our dirt-streaked faces. "You've been digging again," Mom sighed.

"We found what we were looking for," I told her. "We shouldn't have to dig anymore."

"I'm *very* glad to hear it."

Mrs. Bonnycastle had to wait while we washed in the lake and had something to eat. Macaroni and cheese disappeared down Tim's throat like magic. "What do you think Mrs. Bonnycastle wants?" I asked him nervously. "Are we going to say anything about finding the bones?"

"I dunno."

"I wish we could talk to Cass. Now, remember," I told Hugo, "we're not going to say anything to Mrs. Bonnycastle about Paul putting that stuff under the rock."

"I'm not gonna lie," said Hugo through a mouthful of food. "I get mixed up."

The way it worked out, we didn't get a chance to talk

207

to Cass because we all went together in Naomi's van. We had to wing it.

Mrs. Bonnycastle was waiting for us in the big living room. Roger and Anne-Sophie were on the couch beside her, but there was no sign of Mr. Bonnycastle. Paul was over in the corner. He looked glum and his headset was on again. By the time everybody found a seat, Cass ended up sitting beside him.

I figured Mrs. Bonnycastle must have used the delay to refresh her lipstick because it was brighter than ever. Her eyebrows were blacker and sharper. "Thank you for coming at such short notice," she said, but she didn't sound very grateful. She rearranged her skirt and folded her hands. "What I have to say won't be pleasant, but I believe it is important to be honest." She glanced pointedly at Paul. "I try to do what I can for others, and it is disappointing when my consideration is not returned."

Paul drummed his fingers to the music.

"I would have expected you young people to come and ask my permission before you began doing damage to my land," Mrs. Bonnycastle went on. "I've invited you to visit here anytime. *Anytime.* How difficult would it have been for you to approach me? I was very unhappy to learn that you had gone to that silly little newspaper to stir up trouble. And now other reporters are calling me."

The door opened and Mr. Bonnycastle came in. He tiptoed across the room, his shoes squeaking, and sat on the other end of the couch from his wife. "Excuse me, everyone," he whispered loudly. "Held up on the phone."

Mrs. Bonnycastle frowned at him and continued. "The media is very excited about this so-called *sacred* site. All of us in this room know it is nothing of the kind. My own sister's son is behind this foolish, foolish nonsense. The so-called great discovery that you children convinced that girl from *The Beaver* you had made—everything was stolen from this house!"

"We didn't know that then," said Cass. "We didn't know until Mr. Bonnycastle told us."

Mrs. Bonnycastle went on as if Cass hadn't spoken. "I have two choices. I can tell these reporters the truth—that there is nothing special about that land. That there is nothing to prove that godforsaken piece of swamp is different from any other. That it is only a story cooked up among children manipulated by my nephew and an old fool who pretends to be an Indian."

Was she talking about Marcel?

Naomi spoke up angrily. "Excuse me, Helene, but my daughter just told you they had no idea their find wasn't legitimate."

Mrs. Bonnycastle held up her hand. "I am not finished. My other choice is to refuse to talk with the press. You can all do the same. We can get on with our summer plans, and I will not have to send Paul away in disgrace."

She was blackmailing us! I couldn't believe it—in front of our mothers, too! And she was using Paul to do it. Poor Paul. I didn't want him to have to go away.

"Helene, my dear, this is unnecessary," Mr. Bonnycastle said uneasily. "You're within your rights to do whatever you want with your land, but don't go blaming Paul for the mix-up."

Paul's head came up in surprise.

"I've just got off the phone with the police," Mr. Bonnycastle continued. "They've recovered some of the property taken from our house. Not all of it—some has been disposed of, and of course the native artifacts have been recovered. But they have enough to lay charges."

Paul took off his headset.

"They have caught the thieves?" Mrs. Bonnycastle asked.

"Yes, my dear, and I'm afraid you're in for a bit of a shock. You're well acquainted with them. Two local men with records for breaking and entering. Matt Hogan and Leonard Mitchell."

Mom gasped. "Those two! They're the ones who were supposed to be fixing up my studio."

Mrs. Bonnycastle's face was very pale against her vivid lipstick. "This is very distressing. Those men have worked for me for years. Why, even now—I hired them to clear the trailer-park site."

"Then *that's* how the pieces from your father's collection got there!" said Mr. Bonnycastle.

"I can't believe it," she said faintly.

Paul leaned forward. "Did they tell the police that, Uncle Howard? Did they say they put the stolen stuff over there?"

"They claim to have no idea how those things got there. However, they have admitted to taking them from the library. I think we can put one and one together."

"But that's not—" Paul began. Cass kicked him and he muffled a cry of pain.

Mrs. Bonnycastle didn't notice. "So that is the explanation. But it still proves nothing. It's no more a sacred site than I am."

"Yes, it is, Mama," said Roger.

Mrs. Bonnycastle pursed her lips. "Darling, you don't know what we're talking about."

Anne-Sophie pulled on her arm. "He does, Mama. He found out from the Internet."

Mrs. Bonnycastle seemed to be silently counting to ten. She closed her eyes, then opened them. "My son is a computer genius," she explained to everyone.

"It wasn't hard," Roger said. "I did a search under 'Indians' and different ways of spelling 'Algonkin.' And other words, like 'priests.'" He shot me a glance.

"I don't think you understand what we're talking about, *chéri*," his mother repeated more sharply.

"I do," Roger insisted. "I found a website from France, about when the Jesuit priests were missionaries in Canada. It says there was a camp on a lake where nearly all the people died of smallpox, hundreds of them, and it shows a map of our lake. Only I didn't find it at first, because Wasamak's spelled a different way, with an *Ou* at the start, not a *W*. And remember those people that came from the university last year, Mama? They have a website that says the same thing."

Mr. Bonnycastle leaned toward him. "I wasn't aware of that, Roger. Of the website or the information."

"They only put up it up a little while ago. I've been e-mailing them."

"We can talk about all this later, dear," Mrs. Bonnycastle said impatiently. "Mama has more to say."

But now Cass interrupted her. "What's really amazing is that our friend Marcel went to Montreal and found out the same thing as Roger—that there's a lot of people buried there."

"I don't believe a word Marcel Campbell says," Mrs. Bonnycastle cried. "Don't let that old fox pull the wool over your eyes. He pretends to be some kind of Indian shaman, some old wise man, but he lived in Montreal most of his life and made a fortune. He tries to tell me that my property belongs to him, and when he finds out he is mistaken, he thinks he can get at me another way. All the business of websites proves nothing. It is more of his tricks."

"No, it's not, Aunt Helene," said Paul.

Mrs. Bonnycastle tried to talk over him, but he went on. "We've proved it. Just this afternoon. We found bones."

Mr. Bonnycastle sat bolt upright. "Bones? Human bones? You're sure, Paul?"

"Yeah, a leg. We stopped after we got to the foot. But there are lots more."

Mom and Naomi looked shocked. The anger on Mrs. Bonnycastle's face turned to uncertainty and dismay.

Mr. Bonnycastle checked his watch. "We have an hour of daylight left. I suppose it's too late to head over now?"

"Yes!" All three mothers spoke together. I looked at Cass and she rolled her eyes. Trust them to all agree on this.

"If those bones have been there for three hundred years, Howard, they'll be there in the morning," Mrs. Bonnycastle snapped.

Twenty-six

WE WERE GETTING READY FOR BED when Cass rapped on the screen door. "You know you don't need to knock, Cass," Mom told her.

"I wasn't sure anybody here was speaking to me."

"I am," said Hugo.

Mom brushed a bit of cobweb out of Cass's hair. "I thought you all handled yourselves superbly tonight. That couldn't have been easy for you."

"Thanks." Cass still seemed uncomfortable, shifting from foot to foot. I saw her look around for Tim, but he was in his room. "Could we go sit on your porch for a while, Leia?"

I followed her out and we sat. She was being super-nice—she even let me have the rocking chair. I was so stiff from all the digging that I wondered if I'd be able to get out of it again.

Cass stared out at the lake for a while. I waited. Then she cleared her throat. "I want to apologize to you for my behavior." Her voice sounded shaky.

I didn't have the energy to deal with her being upset. "That's okay," I said. "You didn't mean it."

"Don't say that, Leia." She was close to tears. "It's *not* okay. Just 'cause you're nice and don't hold grudges is no reason for me to give you grief." I tried to stop her, but she plowed on. "I don't ever think about anyone's feelings but my own. I'm like a train wreck waiting to happen. No wonder Amy couldn't stand me. I wanted to be different with you guys, and now I've ruined everything."

"It's okay, Cass. We don't need to talk about it any-more."

"It's not okay. You're so *adult* about things. You *think* first. I just rush in and shoot my mouth off. No wonder Tim hates me."

"Tim doesn't hate you! Well...you do irritate him sometimes," I conceded, "but that's just because you have totally different personalities."

"Dad says I antagonize people. I'm such a jerk."

"You're not. You just care about things so much. I think that's good."

"You do?" She finally smiled a little. "Really? You're not just saying that?"

"Really."

She sighed. "You're a great friend, Leia."

"So are you."

We sat there for a while, quietly, both gazing at the lake as the sun set. A heron flapped slowly past on a twilight patrol. Cass sighed again. "Seems like the summer's going really fast, eh?"

"It's only the start of August."

"But you'll be gone the end of next week."

"There's next summer. Lots of summers."

"I really, really hope so." She got up and hugged me, leaning awkwardly over my chair. "Ooof, my poor back." She straightened up. "I'm going to change, Leia. I'll be dif-ferent from now on," she promised.

"Not too different. Then you wouldn't be Cass." Then I laughed. "And I wouldn't be Miss Goody Two-shoes."

"Omigod, I really called you Miss Goody Two-shoes!" She clapped herself on the forehead and made a face. "Where did *that* come from? *The Wizard of Oz* or what?"

"No—that was ruby slippers. Goody Ruby Shoes!" That set us both off giggling. We were so tired we could hardly stop.

Finally Cass wiped her eyes. "Anyway, sorry. I'd better go and let you get to bed. I'm kind of nervous about tomorrow, aren't you? I don't know what's going to happen."

"Fingers crossed."

As she headed back inside, Tim came out of his room. "Hey, Cass."

She paused warily.

"That was a good kick you landed over at the Bonnycastles' tonight," Tim said.

Her face lit up. "Did you see that? I just wanted to shut Paul up."

"Yeah. Saved everybody a lot of trouble."

They stood there for a couple of seconds. Then Cass shook herself and stumbled out the door.

By the time I got finished in the bathroom, the boys' lights were out. Mom was in the kitchen working on her laptop. I stood behind her and put my arms around her neck. "It's late, Mom. You can do that in the morning."

"I know. I'll shut down in a minute."

I set my chin on her head. I wanted to say something and I wasn't sure how she was going to react. "What if— what if I didn't go to Dad's for the whole three weeks, Mom? What if I only went for a week or so? Could I come back here? You wouldn't have to drive all the way down to get me or anything. I could take a bus, right?"

She took her hands off the keyboard and turned to face me. "Don't you want to see your dad?"

"Of course I do. I *love* Dad. And I don't want to hurt his feelings. But I want to come back here, too."

"What about all your friends in Port Hope?"

"They're usually away in the summer anyway." Besides, Tim and Dad would be too busy building some house project for us to go anywhere interesting like Canada's Wonderland. Hugo wouldn't mind—he could

215

skateboard and get in lots of quality television time. The three of them could do some male bonding.

"It's between you and your father, honey," said Mom. "You call Dad and discuss it with him. But if you want to come back here early, I'd love to have you."

As I shuffled off to bed, she called after me. "Are you okay about those bones?"

"Yeah." And I was. Making up with Cass made me feel better about everything.

All night long, though, I dreamed of lying side by side with those people under the rock. I could hear them whispering and murmuring around me, and I tried and tried to make out what they were saying, but I couldn't. It wasn't actually a scary dream, just really sad.

In the morning after breakfast we went over in the boat to meet Mr. Bonnycastle at the site. I'd asked him if Marcel could come, too, and Mr. Bonnycastle said he'd pick him up on the way. He knew the road into Marcel's cabin. Mrs. Bonnycastle refused to join us, but Paul came along. So did Roger.

Marcel climbed stiffly out of the front seat of Mr. Bonnycastle's big green Volvo and waved at us. His old overalls were quite a contrast to Mr. Bonnycastle's white shirt and uncreased trousers. They made their way from the road across to the site, Roger trailing behind.

All our weeks of digging had made a huge mess of the place, heaps of earth and holes everywhere like an infestation of giant groundhogs. We'd left in a hurry the day before, unsettled by our discovery. Tim and Paul had covered the bones with a towel and then a layer of earth, setting rocks on top so no animals could dig them up.

It was a cloudy day but sort of breathless. Mr. Bonnycastle mopped his face with a white handkerchief, watching intently while Tim and Paul cleared away the loose earth in the hole, now several feet deep. Roger stood at the edge beside his father, clutching a map he'd printed from the archeology students' website.

When Paul drew back the towel, there was the long bone with the smaller bones of the ankle and foot at the end of it. A leg—no doubt about it. "Do you want us to dig some more?" he asked. He wasn't smiling or frowning. It was hard to figure out what he was feeling.

"Perhaps you could remove some earth to the left. Please," Mr. Bonnycastle added.

Paul set to work, and Tim cleared the loosened dirt away. We didn't have to wait very long before another big bone appeared. From the angle it didn't seem like it could belong to the same skeleton as the first ones.

Paul worked in silence, his T-shirt darkening with sweat. Nobody talked, except for Mr. Bonnycastle, directing the digging.

Now Paul was clearing earth from another bone. To me it looked like part of a skull.

"An infant, I believe," said Mr. Bonnycastle.

The more they dug, the more bones appeared, big and small, all crowded and crushed together. I closed my eyes and then opened them again. It was like the earth was a curtain, the edge pulled back for a glimpse of what happened here.

I felt a terrible sadness—the same as the very first time I looked through our cottage window out at the lake. Of course, all these people had died long, long ago. Even if they hadn't got smallpox, they'd have been dead three hundred years. But how awful it must have been for them, with their parents, grandparents, sisters and brothers and friends sick and dying all around them. And nobody knowing any way to stop it.

Tim and Hugo got chicken pox, but what if it had been smallpox? And they didn't die—we just got extra holidays.

Paul finally stopped. His hair was soaked. He wiped his face, leaving a muddy trail on his cheek. "Is this enough?"

"For now, yes. Thank you, Paul." Mr. Bonnycastle mopped his face again. "There's already evidence of at least five bodies."

Marcel hadn't been saying anything. Now he spoke up. "Many, many more, I t'ink."

Roger held out the map. "It's right where this says it is, Dad."

His father took it. "Thanks, Roger. I don't need more convincing—we've found the mass grave."

"What are we going to do now, Mr. Bonnycastle?" Cass asked.

He thought a minute. "Proceed with caution. Contact the university, I suppose."

"Tell the band council," said Paul.

"Yes," said his uncle reluctantly. "Of course, as soon as we do that, it will likely mean the end of the digging. They won't want any further disturbance of the dead. But we must be careful to do the right thing."

We were all still crouched at the edge of the pit. "It's a sobering sight," Mr. Bonnycastle said. "I hope it hasn't upset any of you. It may make you feel better to hear that my wife won't be proceeding with her project."

It took a moment for the words to sink in. "She won't?" We all spoke more or less together, and Mr. Bonnycastle laughed a little at the shocked looks on our faces.

I opened my mouth to whoop, then shut it. "But you told us before that if she couldn't build here, she'd just move the trailer park farther along the shore," I reminded him.

He shook his head. "The land there is too damp and low-lying. It would mean a lot of dredging and infilling. And since that story appeared in *The Beaver*, we've been hearing from the lake association and the local naturalists group. They're concerned about the loss of wetlands."

Cass grinned. "Good old Dad! I bet he's responsible for some of that. He said he was going to make some calls about his least bittern."

Paul covered the bones again, and we all helped him shovel the rest of the dirt back into the hole. When it was smoothed over, Mr. Bonnycastle checked his watch. "Nothing more to be done here for the moment. I should be getting home. Can I offer you a ride back, Marcel?"

"No, t'anks. I'll make my own way."

"I'll stay, too, Uncle Howard," said Paul.

"How will you get home?"

"We can take him back by boat," Cass said.

"Maybe Roger wants to stay, too," said Hugo.

Roger looked surprised. "Not right now. I might another time." It sounded stiff, but I could tell he was pleased to be asked. Good for Hugo.

"I'll come and play with your Xbox some time," he added generously.

We went out to the road and watched Mr. Bonnycastle's car leave. Roger gave a self-conscious wave. Then we walked back to the site, not saying much. We were all feeling a bit stunned.

"Hey, Leia, there's your towel," Hugo said. It was the one that Paul used to cover the bones, thrown aside on the grass and gray with dirt like an ancient rag. "You'd better wash it before Mom sees."

"Just leave it." I couldn't imagine ever wanting to use that towel again. "Mom won't mind."

"We can burn it," said Cass. "Make it part of a ceremony, once we've put the place back the way it was."

"And after that, no one should disturb it," Paul said firmly.

"Those archeology guys from the university are going to want to for sure," said Tim.

"We'll see what the band council has to say about that."

Cass was gazing at the flattened earth. "So...that means we've done it," she said, as if she couldn't believe it. "Doesn't it? Isn't that right? I still can't get my brain around it. Or is there something bad I've forgotten?"

"No," said Marcel. "You should be proud, all of you, what you done."

"Mrs. Bonnycastle isn't going to build a trailer park on Half Moon Bay!" Cass threw her arms around him. "Isn't it fantastic?"

Marcel smiled broadly. "Dat make me feel a whole lot happier, I admit."

It was amazing. We'd tried so hard, and now we could hardly accept that we'd won.

"It's just too bad this won't make any difference to the rest of the lake," Cass went on. "Wish we could figure out a way to save that."

"Seem like we can't stop progress," Marcel said. "Only we can maybe slow it down. An' respect de past an' what has come before us. Like you did."

Paul was standing off to one side. He didn't seem as happy as the rest of us. "Are you feeling bad about digging up those people?" I asked him.

"I didn't like it much. But I got into it," he admitted. "I guess if I were those people, I wouldn't mind being dug up. I mean, one time, if I knew it was going to do some good."

220

"And it did," said Marcel.

"Yeah. But they shouldn't be bothered anymore."

"I agree," said Cass. "We should be the guardians of this place from now on."

"I been t'inking about that, too," Marcel said. He didn't say anything more, though. I guess he was still thinking.

"About what?" Cass prompted.

"I t'ink...soon as I get clear title to my part of dis swampland sorted out, I t'ink I give it to some guardian."

"Give it away?" I cried, dismayed.

"Just keep it yourself, the way it is," Cass said.

"Okay for now. But what happen to it after I'm gone?"

He was old, he meant. Seventy, or even older. He wouldn't live forever. I didn't want to think about that. Marcel wasn't going to die for a long time yet.

"At first I was t'inking, maybe I give it to some organization to care for," he went on. "Keep it safe. Make sure nobody else try to pave it over. But now...I got another idea. Maybe better one. Maybe I give it to somebody who keep it Algonkin land."

"The band council, you mean?" said Paul.

Marcel shrugged. "Maybe not. Maybe one person I know. I jus' t'ink of it now."

He was looking straight at Paul. Right away I knew what he was getting at. He wasn't talking about the band council. Marcel was talking about giving his land to Paul.

Cass saw it, too. "Oh, great! That's brilliant! That'll drive his aunt completely nuts!"

Finally Paul got it. "You mean me?" he stammered. "You want to give it to me?" Like he was the last person in the world anybody would consider.

"I t'ink you be a good guardian. But you got lots of time to decide. I got no plans to die soon. I still got plenty to do."

221

"That reminds me," Cass said slowly. She was staring at Marcel, her eyes narrowed. "You know what Mrs. Bonnycastle tried to tell us, Marcel? Something really strange. She said you used to live in Montreal and made a lot of money. How weird is that?"

Marcel scratched his beard. Then he nodded. "It is true. For long time I have a different life from now."

"What did you do?" I asked.

"Build t'ings."

"*Build* things?" Cass cried. "What kind of things?"

"Subdivision, high rise."

Cass's mouth fell open. "But—how could you? That can't be true. You can't build things without knowing a lot of math and science and all that."

"True," he agreed. "Otherwise what I build falls down."

"So where did you learn all that?"

"School of engineering."

She quivered with indignation. "You mean you went to college? Or university? You lied to us, Marcel! You let us think you were just an old hermit who lives in the woods."

"Never said I was an old 'ermit. Now, yes, I am. At least, learning to be one." He returned Cass's glare with a grin. "You don't like an old fool 'aving a little joke?"

"No!" she retorted, hands on her hips. "Adults are supposed to set an example, not go around playing tricks on people."

"Is that so?" he raised his eyebrows. "I never see much of that in my life. I never tol' a lie," he pointed out. "Well, maybe I stretch the trut' a bit."

"I don't mind," Hugo said generously. "I like it when grown-ups play tricks." He pulled on my arm. "Can we go home now and swim? I'm *broiling*."

As everyone started toward the boat, Marcel turned

onto a narrow ridge that ran across the wet ground. "I go dis way. Come tomorrow an' we celebrate, okay? No champagne, but you know I make good coffee." He waved and headed off.

All five of us managed to fit in the aluminum boat—Cass in the stern, Tim in the bow, and Paul, me and Hugo in the middle. As we all got settled, my leg bumped Paul's. We both said sorry, but the seat was so crowded that we had to sit with our knees touching. I didn't mind at all.

Cass started the motor and reversed up the channel. I was looking past her, out to the bay. The sun had come out, and the light glinted off the little waves on the water. And there, perfectly framed by the bulrushes, was a loon. Behind it two smaller loon heads appeared, sticking close by the parent.

Then I remembered back to when I saw them from our dock—was it just yesterday morning? It seemed a million years ago, after the way everything had changed. In all the excitement of the digging and Mrs. Bonnycastle's big showdown and our incredible discovery, I'd forgotten something—something really important.

I pointed. "Cass, look! The loon chicks hatched after all!"